TRINITY ACADEMY

M⊛S O N

Cover Designer: Sybil Wilson, PopKitty Design

Cover Model: Forest

Photographer Credit: Wander Book Club Photography

TABLE OF CONTENTS

Dedication

Kelly, Sheena & Sherrie

Thank you for always challenging me,
and for helping to grow as an author.
I'm so damn grateful for each one of you.

Songlist

NF - <u>Paralyzed</u>

Brighton – <u>Forest Fire</u>

Lewis Capaldi – <u>Someone You Loved</u>

HAEVN – <u>We Are</u>

Synopsis

"You're my assistant."

The magic words every girl at Trinity Academy is dying to hear.

But I'm the one who gets stuck with Mason Chargill, the star of most women's fantasies but my nightmare. One of the heirs to CRC Holdings, he might be dangerously gorgeous, but his cold and callous demeanor makes him an ice prince.

He expects me to abide by the Academy's hierarchy, to be at his constant beck and call.
Yeah, right… hell will freeze over before that ever happens.

Unfortunately for him, I'm no pushover.
Unfortunately for me, he's determined to break me.

If only there were a way to melt that shard of ice, he calls a heart.

Prologue

Please read Falcon before continuing with Mason
as all the books in this series are interconnected.

Mason

(Seventeen-years old.)

"How bad is this weather tonight?" Jennifer asks while we're driving home after having dinner at Falcon's house. "Oh! I almost forgot. I have a song I want you to listen to."

My eyes shift from my phone to my sister. "Is it another one of those sappy ones?"

Jennifer smiles, knowing I'm only teasing her. "I'm willing to bet anything you'll like this one."

Picking up her phone, while her eyes keep glancing at the road, she looks for the song, and a moment later, guitar strings sound up. It's a lazy melody at first. Jennifer grins at me when whistling joins the strings, and she reaches for the radio to turn up the volume.

When the car swerves on the icy road, she quickly grabs hold of the steering wheel with both hands. "It's really bad out," she mutters while her face is strained with worry. The words have hardly left her mouth when the car's tail end begins to pull to the left. "Shit, Mace, I've lost traction!"

As Jen taps the breaks, I reach over to the steering wheel, but she snaps, "It won't help. The road is too icy."

The car keeps gliding, and when it's diagonally in the road, bright lights fall on us.

"We need to move!" Fear prickles over the back of my head as my heart begins to pound out of control.

Fuck, they're going to hit us.

The other vehicle tries to slow down, but they drive over the same patch of black ice.

"Fu-uuck!" A second later, they crash into my side of the car. "Jen!" a shout rips from my chest as our car begins to spin across the road.

"Shit. Shit. Shit," she whispers as we uncontrollably spin into oncoming traffic. Flinging my left arm across Jennifer's chest, I try to brace her for the unavoidable impact.

Jennifer's side takes the full brunt of the blow as a vehicle collides with ours, and the impact sends our car shooting backward.

"Mace!" Jennifer lets go of the steering wheel, and grabs hold of my arm with both her hands.

It feels like the worst rollercoaster ride of my life as our car pivots sharply before coming to a sudden standstill as it crashes into a tree. The windshield shatters, and I can hear pieces of glass and metal falling. I quickly glance at Jennifer, and when her wide eyes meet mine, I feel a moment of relief. We both look down at the branch that crashed through our windshield but luckily stopped within inches of my arm.

"Fuck, that was close." My voice sounds hoarse from the horrific moment we just lived through.

"Yeah," Jennifer whispers.

I begin to pull my left arm back, but the sound of squealing tires has me glancing behind us. I only have a second to react, and I throw my body to the left, trying to reach for the branch.

Our bodies are jolted forward, and I manage to keep my arm braced over Jennifer, with my fist tightly gripping hold of her sweater. A sharp pain pierces through my left arm before I'm slammed back against my seat, the sudden movement stunning my senses.

Dazed, I mumble, "Fuck." I try to pull my arm back, but when it doesn't move, apprehension slithers through me.

It feels like time itself hesitates, but when I hear a gurgling sound, it's forced to speed along.

In absolute terror, I turn my head toward Jennifer. The sight looks disturbingly peaceful as horror and anguish begin to war inside of me.

Her cheek is resting on the branch as if she just leaned forward and decided to fall asleep.

"Jen, wake up," I stupidly whisper.

One breath.

Two beats of my heart.

My entire world – everything that represented home and family – warps into an unrecognizable mess.

Blood trickles from her mouth, and I hear the gurgling sound again. I can only sit paralyzed, my eyes wide on my sister.

Slowly, the cold creeps into my bones, and I gasp for a breath of icy air. Scared out of my mind, I raise my right hand and reach out to Jennifer. The moment my fingers brush over her cheek, and I feel some warmth in her skin, I lunge toward her, only to be restrained by the safety belt.

"Jen!" Her name explodes harshly over my lips. Her eyelashes flutter and needing to get to my sister, I struggle to unclasp the safety belt and manage to free myself. But when I lunge forward again, I'm stopped by the branch pinning me to her chest. A jarring ache spreads through my left arm and up into my shoulder.

She gasps for air, instantly drawing my attention away from the pain.

My right hand trembles uncontrollably as my fingers brush over her forehead. "Jen?"

Somehow my instincts kick in, and I fumble for my phone, so I can call emergency services, but I can't find it, and it makes desperation crush my heart.

"Jennifer!" I cry, disoriented by the harrowing inability to help my sister.

"Jennifer!"

I should have yanked her to me.

"Jennifer!"

No. No. No. No. No.

This isn't happening.

This isn't real.

Chapter 1

Mason

(Twenty-two-years old / Present day.)

"My ears are freezing. They feel like two blocks of ice," Kingsley complains.

I resist the urge to tell her it's because she's wearing that shitty excuse for a headband instead of a decent balaclava. The guys are already pissed with me for being confrontational with Kingsley, so I try to save face by stepping up behind her.

When I push her hands away, Kingsley scowls, "What are you doing?"

Already regretting my decision to be nice, I ignore her. I cover her ears and lean forward. Blowing hot air between my cupped hand and her ear, I'm hoping it will shut her up for a couple of minutes.

But my hope is short-lived as she asks, "Ahh… what's happening right now?"

Fuck my life, it's hard to not give in to the temptation to shove her face first down into the snow.

"I'm being nice," I mutter, then quickly warm her other ear before I adjust the headband. I almost slap her on the back but stop myself in time and give her a quick pat instead.

Noticing the ski lifts are coming in, I move toward it before I die of an overdose of her perky attitude.

The only thing I like perky is a nice pair of...

"Should I worry?" Kingsley asks, making my irritation increase. "Do you think maybe he's lost his mind?"

You can't hit a girl.

You can't hit a girl.

You can't hit a girl.

I'm struggling as is, then Lake adds, "I'm actually not sure."

Fuckers.

All of them.

Right before stepping up to the lift, I glare at them. "See, when I'm nice, you all think I'm insane. Get your asses to the lifts, so I can push Hunt down the slope." I sit my ass down, muttering, "Can't fucking win."

"He's fine," Falcon says.

14

Going up, I zone out, not taking in any of the nature around me.

Why the fuck am I torturing myself like this?

Oh, yeah. Because it's for Layla, and Falcon loves the girl.

My thoughts go back to yesterday when Layla hugged me. She totally caught me off guard. I'm used to people scattering away from me. Definitely not hugging me and telling me to breathe.

I get why Falcon fell for her. Her balls to the wall attitude alone is enough to catch your attention, never mind her ability to make you feel calm and at home.

Home.

I haven't felt that in a long time. Sure, I have Falcon and Lake, but there's just something different a woman brings to a household.

Warmth. Tenderness.

I lost that five years ago, and since Layla started dating Falcon, I've seen glimpses of it, and it's been blinding me.

Add Kingsley's overexcited, happy go lucky attitude, and I'm ready to dig my eyes out.

They remind me of what I've lost, and seeing as I can't tell Layla to fuck off, I direct my anger at Kingsley.

15

Reaching the top of the slope, I get off and walk over to the benches so I can put on my gear. I take my time, letting the others go ahead of me.

I'm really not in the mood for this, but I get up and ski closer to where Lake is.

"Oh shit. Oh shit. Oh shit," Kingsley panics. She's about to lose her balance, so I slowly ski up behind her and placing my hands on her hips, I help her to remain standing.

Fulfilling my 'being nice' quota for the day, I ski away from her and shout, "Try not to break your neck, Hunt."

Skiing down the slope, the wind rushes past me, and when I reach the bottom, I'm tempted to say fuck it and to head to the resort. But because my friends are up on the slope, I head over to the lift and make my way back up to them.

An hour later, Kingsley's arms wave wildly at her sides as she tries to keep her balance where she's skiing at a snail's pace slightly in front of me. I plant my poles in the snow and grabbing hold of her hips, I help her to regain her balance. She turns her head, and when she sees me, her eyes widen behind the pink Oakley goggles.

"Why are you still surprised, Hunt? It's like the fiftieth time already. Next time, I'm letting you eat snow," I growl,

16

maddened by her uncanny ability to aggravate me with just one look.

I take hold of my poles and watch as Lake skis toward us. Once again, he's not able to stop, which causes him to plow into Kingsley. A grin spreads over my face until I hear her laugh. The sound has my eye fucking twitching as if I'm about to have a damn stroke.

Her cheerfulness is bound to kill me.

She's always smiling as if life is nothing but unicorn farts and butterflies shitting all over the fucking flowers. It irritates the living fuck out of me.

I hold a hand out to Lake, and once he grabs hold of it, I pull him up.

"Thanks," he breathes, reaching up to his face to adjust his goggles. "All this snow is making me hungry. Are we going to head back down?"

"Don't use the snow for an excuse to eat." I grin at him. "Yeah, let's go feed that bottomless fucking pit you call a stomach."

Anything to get off this damn slope and away from Kingsley.

Lake turns to Kingsley, but I grab hold of his arm, and when he glances back to me, I shake my head. "Don't. I need a break from her."

17

Lake shrugs, and after helping Kingsley up, he begins to slowly ski down the slope. Just as I'm about to push away, Kingsley asks, "Where's Lake going?"

I almost answer her but decide it's not worth my time.

"Avalanche!" a skier yells from higher up, making my gaze dart up the slope.

As I turn my head back in Lake's direction, my eyes skim over Kingsley. Spotting Lake, I shout, "Lake, Avalanche! Warn Falcon!"

A wave of snow washes my feet from under me, knocking me backward. I hear Kingsley scream, and instinctively I fling my left arm in her direction. I manage to grab hold of her jacket and try to yank her toward me. Chunks of ice keep coming, pushing us forward before I can get Kingsley to me, and the damn glove makes it hard to hold on to her.

"Fuck!" I shout when I feel her jacket slip from my hold. I'm inundated with snow and let it take me, knowing there's no fighting it. It pushes me another hundred yards before I finally come to a stop.

Struggling, all I can hear are my breaths before I finally manage to sit up. "Lake! Falcon!"

My eyes sweep over the mess of disoriented skiers, all calling out names of loved ones they got separated from.

When I don't see either of my friends, I begin to shout their names repeatedly. It takes a lot of effort to get myself back on my feet. With the snow broken up, it's harder to move, but I manage to make progress as I keep calling, "Falcon! Lake!"

"Mason," Falcon shouts from behind me. I glance up and feel some relief when I see him helping Layla to her feet.

Cupping my hands around my mouth, I call to him, "Can you see Lake?"

"No!"

"Fuck," I mutter, and looking over all the people, I make sure I didn't miss him before I set my poles aside. I take off my skies and place them next to the poles, then shrug off my backpack.

Worry crawls over my body as I call loudly, "Lake!"

I focus on an area and shout his name again. I keep doing this while moving across the fractured snow. "Fucking answer me!" Panic closes over my heart, and I feel the familiar horrible sting of hopelessness.

Suddenly a pole shoots up through a bank of snow, and I call out his name again to make sure it's him. The pole moves, and I quickly turn to where I last saw Falcon. "Lake's over here! He's buried!"

Knowing minutes have already passed, I try to run, but the fucking snow keeps giving way beneath my feet, and I fall to my knees. Not wanting to waste any more time, I crawl the rest of the way, and when I reach the pole, I begin to dig as fast as I can. After I've cleared quite a bit away, and I still haven't reached him, I shout, "I've got you, Lake."

"Hold on, buddy."

"Please."

Falcon drops down next to me and begins to shovel snow away. We work as fast as we can, and when my hand slams into something hard, I feel a wave of dizzying elation. I clear the snow away from his helmet and at last get to his face.

"Can you breathe?" Falcon asks him, pausing for a moment to check on Lake.

I can't bring myself to stop and keep shoveling snow away until his entire upper body is free. Falcon grabs Lake under his arms and pulls him free, and all I can do is sit back while gasping for air.

"Oh, God," Layla whimpers behind me. I don't even have the strength to glance up at her. "Lake, are you okay?" The worry in her voice grates at my nerves, which feel like they've been put through a grinder.

"Are you hurt?" Falcon asks, keeping his hand on Lake's shoulder.

"I'm good." Lake takes deep breaths, pressing a hand to his chest. "Just need air."

The relief I feel when I meet his eyes is only short-lived and is quickly replaced by paralyzing fear. In absolute terror, I turn my head to where I last had a hold of Kingsley.

The sight of the white snow looks disturbingly peaceful as horror and anguish begin to war inside of me. It feels as if I'm being sucked into the past when the realization hits – I don't see Kingsley.

"Kingsley," I stupidly whisper.

A feeling of Deja Vu eerily ripples over me.

One breath.

Two beats of my heart.

My carefully patched up world – everything that's been keeping my sanity from snapping – warps into chaos.

"What did you say?" Falcon asks, and leaning forward, he must catch sight of the look in my eyes, because he instantly kneels down in front of me. "What's wrong?"

I shake my head to get out of the paralyzing daze I'm caught in. "Kingsley. I couldn't hold on to her."

"Oh, God," Layla gasps, and I almost snap at her to shut up.

I grab hold of Falcon's shoulder and use him, so I can climb to my feet.

How long has it been? Ten minutes? An hour?

I struggle back to where my stuff is and feeling utterly exhausted, I close my eyes. I take a deep breath and squaring my shoulders, I cup my hands around my mouth and shout, "Kingsley!"

I don't bother with the people either making their way to the ski lifts or skiing down the slope. I don't check to see what Falcon and Lake are doing.

I begin to search, feebly hoping she's not buried under the snow.

I should have held onto her.

The second I knew of the avalanche, I should've grabbed her to me instead of just letting my eyes pass over.

Another feeling of Deja Vu eerily flutters through me, yanking me back into the past.

I could have saved her.

She's dead because of me.

Chapter 2

Kingsley

Waking, half-covered in snow, I'm blinded by the sun reflecting off the fresh powder.

I let out a groan then lift my head. Not seeing anything familiar, I pull my right hand from where it's stuck beneath me and let out a painful cry when sharp pain cuts through my wrist. I suck in a couple of icy breaths before I carefully try to turn onto my back, but the movement only engulfs my right ankle in pain.

"Crap, it hurts," I groan, keeping still until the aching subsides a little.

It's so cold.

Using my left arm, I push myself into a sitting position and shake the snow off of me. Remembering the avalanche, I hurriedly glance around me. Panic slams hard into me when I realize the snow pushed me into a lining of trees, and I have no idea where I am. I can't see anyone. A ski sticks out of the ice a couple of feet away, and further up, I catch sight of a pole.

Damn, I lost everything on the way down.

I sit still for a couple of minutes, processing the situation while trying to come up with a plan.

What do I do now?

Looking down at my right hand, I pull my sleeve up to see if it's bleeding. Luckily, it's only blue and swollen. I probably sprained my wrist and ankle when I landed on it.

"I wish I had my phone," I mutter. "It's the last time I go anywhere without it."

Making the decision to get moving, I put most of my weight on my left hand and leg and grind my teeth against the pain while I climb to my feet. Once I'm standing, I lift my right foot from the snow and glance around me again.

"Which way do I go?"

I look to the sides of me, and then down the mountain.

"I suppose down is best. Getting off the mountain is all that matters." I try to hop, but it's a failure of epic proportions when I just sink deeper into the snow.

"Kingsley!"

I freeze like a deer when I hear Mason's shout.

Now is not the time to be picky about who saves your ass. It's not like you can walk on your own.

24

"Mason?" I call out.

"Kingsley!"

His voice sounds closer, and I turn to my left, this time yelling, "Mason."

I see a glimpse of black a little ways up, and then Mason appears from behind a line of trees.

Sigh. The beauty of a fallen angel... with a soul as dark as night.

He's moving fast, sliding sideways down the steeper patches.

I might not like him, and even though he scares the crap out of me, I have to admit I'm glad to see him. When he's closer, I feel the familiar nervousness which I've become accustomed to whenever he's around, and I begin to ramble, "I have no idea how I ended up out here. One minute I'm standing on the slope with you, and the next it's like bam, I'm out in the sticks." I glance down at my leg. "I think I sprained my ankle. Oh, and my wrist." I hold my wrist up for him to see, and as I look up, my eyes just about pop out of my head.

Mason slams into me, and wrapping his arms around me, he lifts me off the ground with a tight hug.

Okkkkaaayyyy?

25

I still have my hands up in the air, and while I try to decide whether I should hug him back, his body shudders against mine.

"Fuck," he whispers. "I'm so sorry I didn't pull you toward me." His voice is tight with emotion.

I bring my left hand down to his arm and awkwardly pat him. "It's okay."

I glance up the mountain, silently hoping Layla, or anyone else would appear, but I'm fresh out of luck.

"Uhm... where's the rest of the group?"

My question has Mason pulling back. He lets go of me, and when my feet touch the snow, pain shudders through my right ankle, making me lose my balance.

Mason quickly grabs hold of my left arm, and I wait for him to snap at me, but he doesn't. Instead, he glances down at my right leg, which is up in the air.

He doesn't say anything, and when he crouches down in front of me, turning his back to me, I blink stupidly at him.

"Get on, Hunt. I can't carry you and move through the snow. I need my arms free."

"Oh." I place my hand on his shoulder and begin to lean forward.

Well, this isn't awkward at all.

Reaching behind him, Mason takes hold of my thighs and pulls me flush against his back. I let out a surprised squeak and quickly wrap my left arm around his neck.

I'm just about to ask who he is and what he's done with the real Mason, but I swallow the words down when I glance at his face. Usually, Mason looks pissed. But the way his breaths explode over his lips along with the distressed frown between his eyes, it makes him look like a totally different person.

Shit, no!

"Did anyone get hurt?" I blurt out, fearful something bad has happened to one of my friends.

Mason shakes his head and begins to move.

"So, everyone is fine?"

He nods again, then swallows hard.

"Your face tells me something happened," I argue, needing to know the truth.

"Shut up, Hunt," he mutters as if it's taking a lot of effort for him to speak.

A new worry begins to niggle.

What if he hurt himself?

"Are you okay?"

"Kingsley!" he snaps. "Shut the fuck up."

Nope, he's okay. It must be my imagination.

27

When we finally make it to where the rest of the group is, I let out a relieved sigh.

"You found her!" Layla cries, and she begins to stumble through the snow to get to us.

"I better let the search and rescue know," Falcon says, then turns to head over to where a group of people is gathered.

Mason takes hold of my left arm and basically just shrugs me off of his back.

"Oomph!" I hit the snow, and it makes the dull pain in my wrist and ankle roar back to life. "Owwww, Jerk!" I snap at Mason's back, before mumbling, "Thank you."

Layla almost falls over me in her hurry to hug me. I let out a burst of laughter when her arms wrap tightly around my neck. "I was so worried. Thank God, you're okay."

Lake crouches down next to me, giving me a grateful smile.

"I'm glad to see you're all okay," I say.

Lake pats my shoulder, then he gets up and walks over to Mason, who seriously looks like a caged animal.

"Are you okay?" I hear Lake ask Mason.

Mason just stares at Lake, and I don't know what Lake sees, but he turns toward Falcon and yells, "I'm taking Mason down. Let's meet up at the resort."

"We're heading down as well," Falcon answers while he comes back to Layla and me. "Are you good to walk, Kingsley?"

I shake my head, scrunching my nose as I glare down at my foot. "I sprained my ankle."

Falcon bends down and gently picks me up, giving me a reassuring look.

Yep, this is the difference between Falcon and Mason. Falcon treats you like a princess where Mason-the-damn-caveman just tosses you around.

Layla fusses over me all the way down the slope and on the ride to the hospital. I'm surprised Mason and Lake ride with us, thinking they would've gone to the resort.

When we walk into the emergency center, Lake turns to Falcon, "We'll be back soon."

Falcon quickly grabs hold of Mason's arm and glances at Layla and me. "You'll manage, right?"

"Oh, yeah. Sure," Layla answers, her eyes going to Mason, who keeps himself turned away from us.

I tilt my head and frown as the guys walk away. "I'm seriously missing something right now."

Layla places her arm around me, then explains, "They're worried over Mason. I think he's in shock."

I take hold of her with my left hand and begin to hop toward reception.

When I'm all bandaged up, and I have some anti-inflammatory meds, I sit down in the waiting area while Layla goes to look for the guys.

It doesn't take long before I see them walk toward me. Layla and Falcon hang back, talking about something, while Lake heads toward the pharmacy to get a prescription filled out.

Mason comes over to the waiting area and passes right by me. Glancing over my shoulder, I watch him sit down in the furthest seat from me. I'm not going to lie. It stings. I have no idea what I did to make him hate me so much.

Shrugging the negativity away, I glance at Layla and Falcon. They're still talking, so I look down at my bandaged hand.

When Lake is done getting the medication, he comes toward me. "Let's get going." He glances over at Falcon and calls out, "All set. Let's go."

I get up and smile gratefully at Lake when he places an arm around my waist. Leaning on him, I hop toward the exit with his help.

As we walk outside toward the van, I notice Lake holding the medicine out to Mason. But instead of taking it, Mason shakes his head, grumbling, "I'm not taking that shit. I'll be fine."

He then walks ahead of us and staring at the wide expanse of his back, I wonder what the medication is for.

I hope he's okay.

Chapter 3

Mason

Fucking PTSD my ass.

I'm just shaken up by the incident.

Sitting in the back of the van, I stare blankly out of the window. I don't have an appetite, but I know Lake must be starving, and that's the only reason I'm not saying anything when Falcon drives to a restaurant.

"I think I can eat an entire cow," Kingsley says happily as if she didn't get hit by a damn avalanche just a couple of hours ago.

I wish I were back at Trinity.

"Damn, you and me both," Lake chuckles. "Ahh… I can already see the steak." He pauses then begins to add a whole list, "And pizza. And tacos. And chicken wings."

I just want to lie down on my own bed and not get up again.

"So, basically the whole menu," Layla teases him.

I keep smelling the fumes from the car.

"You know me well," Lake chuckles.

I close my eyes, and when the image of Jen slumped over the branch flashes through my mind, suffocating sorrow wells up inside my chest.

"I just want anything warm. It feels like I'm a block of ice," Layla complains.

My eyes catch Falcon's in the rearview mirror, and I quickly lower my head. I turn my face away so he can't see as a tear escapes. Casually, bringing my hand up, I rest my chin on my thumb and wipe the tear away with my knuckles.

Breathe.

Just breathe.

I try to focus on every breath I take, but images keep flashing through my mind.

"We're here. Finally, food!" Lake coos.

Jennifer cheering me on while I'm playing basketball with Falcon and Lake.

"Lake, will you be my hero and give me a piggyback ride?" Kingsley begs.

Jennifer tousling my hair.

Jennifer smiling.

"Mason?" Falcon sits down next to me, and it's a struggle to lift my eyes. "The others have gone to the restaurant." He places his arm behind me and leans forward. When his eyes catch mine, he brings his other arm around me and hugs me to him. "I'm here."

I try to nod, but the emotions leave me feeling dazed and sluggish.

"I'm here, buddy." I'm grateful to him for not asking how I feel.

I wouldn't know how to answer that.

Fucked? Lost? Broken beyond repair?

Falcon sits with me for a while, and it gives me time to push some of the emotions down.

"I suppose we have to head inside," I mutter.

"No, we can sit here until they're done. I don't mind."

This is why I consider him my brother. He's always been there, a silent force keeping me from giving up.

"Let's go eat," I say, willing my voice to sound stronger.

"You sure?" Falcon asks, shifting forward when I gesture for him to move.

"I'm sure." I force a smile to my lips.

I follow Falcon out of the van and into the restaurant. My eyes land on Lake, who freezes with a slice of pizza

34

inches from his mouth, and the sight brings a real smile to my face.

Falcon goes to sit next to Layla, and the smile quickly drops from my face as I glare at Lake when I have to take the seat between him and Kingsley.

"Fucker," I mumble under my breath.

"I needed more space for all the food," Lake explains.

I shake my head, letting out a burst of silent laughter.

"Grab a slice," Lake says right before he stuffs half the damn pizza into his mouth.

A waiter comes to bring more food to the table, and I order a drink, needing something strong to help take the edge off.

As the waiter leaves with my order, Lake grumbles, "You better eat something, or I'm going to force-feed you."

"Shoot," Kingsley mumbles next to me, drawing my attention.

Glancing at her, I watch her brow furrow as she stares longingly at the steak on her plate, gripping a fork in her left hand.

"Clearly, I didn't think this through," she whispers.

I let out a sigh and reach over her, grabbing the fork from her hand while picking up her knife. I cut the steak into small pieces, then drop the cutlery next to the plate.

Luckily, the waiter brings my drink and taking it from him, I say, "Thanks." Bringing the tumbler to my mouth, I take two huge sips. When the whiskey burns down my throat, I almost close my eyes from the relief it makes me feel.

Setting the glass down in front of me, Kingsley whispers, "Thank you."

I don't bother acknowledging her gratitude.

When Lake frowns at me, I reach over and pick a piece of chicken from the slice of pizza on his plate. Popping it into my mouth, I swallow the thing whole, then grumble, "I ate. Chill now."

"It's so damn hard raising kids," Lake mutters, shaking his head. "Won't eat when you tell them to. Won't take their meds when you tell them to. My eldest will be the end of me one of these days. Stubborn fucker."

Kingsley bursts out laughing from what Lake just said, and a piece of steak flies from her mouth, smacking against Falcon's chest.

Falcon almost does a backflip to get away from the half-eaten piece of meat. Layla's laughter explodes through the restaurant as she cracks up while pointing a finger at Falcon.

"Being hit by a flying piece of cow," Falcon states, a serious expression on his face. "Guess there's a first for everything."

Kingsley tilts sideways in her chair from the laughter shaking her. Looking at her, I watch tears spill over her cheeks as she gasps for air, and the realization that she's seriously cute right now hits.

Then she snorts.

Just a moment of insanity, buddy. Nothing to worry about.

When we get back to the cabin, I walk right through to the sliding doors and opening them, I step out onto the deck. I shut the doors behind me and grabbing a chair, I pull it away from the view of the living room. Sitting down, I lean back, and lifting my legs, I rest my feet on the banister.

It's quickly growing dark as I stare at the bare tree a couple of yards away.

'Don't you think it's amazing, Mace?'

'What?'

'The tree.' Jen points at it. *'It looks dead now, but in a couple of months, it will be sprouting new leaves.'*

37

"You didn't get to see it," I whisper.

I close my eyes as waves of pain roll over me.

'Mace, are you okay with it all?'

'With you marrying Julian?'

'Yeah.'

'Of course. As long as you'll be happy, Jen. Plus, it will make Falcon my brother.'

'Technically, Falcon will be my brother-in-law,' she teases.

I roll my eyes at her. 'Duh, that makes him my brother as well.'

"Are you haunting me, Jen?" I say the words softly to the night closing in around me. "Is it because I failed you?"

'I love you, Mace.'

"I keep blaming that fucker for slamming into the back of us." I swallow hard, and just the thought of West Dayton makes rage burn through the grief. "But it's as much my fault, as it is his."

'Yeah,' Jennifer whispers.

I hear the sliding door open and glance up. Falcon and Lake step outside, and then Lake hands me a cup of coffee.

"Fuck, it's cold out here," Falcon says as he pulls a chair closer and sits down. He lifts his feet to the banister.

Lake does the same, and then the three of us stare out into the darkness for a little while.

"I think the last of my coffee just froze," Lake mutters.

I let out a chuckle. "Go inside. You guys really don't have to sit out here."

I hear the sliding door opening again, and glancing up, I see it's Layla with an armful of blankets. "Figured you guys might need these."

She hands Lake one, and he stands up, wrapping the thing around him before falling back into the chair. "You saved my life," he praises her while shivering his ass off.

Layla opens a blanket and places it over Falcon before pressing a kiss to his lips.

Lovingly, he smiles at her. "Thanks, my rainbow."

When she gets to me, I hold my hand out. "You don't have to tuck me in."

Grinning at me, she wags her eyebrows. "You sure about that?"

"Layla," Falcon grumbles, making me smile.

"I'm sure. Thanks," I say before Falcon shits himself, but then add, "Jealous much?"

"Fuck off," he mutters, a smile pulling at his lips.

"Can I make anyone coffee?" Kingsley asks from where she's leaning against the doorjamb.

"God, Kingsley, I'll love you forever," Lake exclaims.

"Please," Falcon says, grabbing hold of Layla's hand before she can head back inside. He pulls her down for another quick kiss, then lets her go.

Still folded, the blanket lies forgotten on my lap.

'Love you,' I hear Jen whisper to Julian.

He presses a kiss to her mouth before she climbs behind the steering wheel.

'Drive safely and text me once you get home.'

She never got to send him that text.

Chapter 4

Kingsley

I was tired, but the moment I crawled into bed, I started thinking about the day.

And Mason's weird behavior.

When I hear footsteps coming toward the room, I quickly turn on my side, so I'm facing the wall, then shut my eyes.

"Try to sleep. You need the rest after searching hours for Kingsley," Lake whispers.

Mason grumbles something I can't make out. They move around the room, and a couple of minutes later, I hear them settling into bed.

I peek at the wall, then almost roll my eyes at myself, because I'm lying with my back to the guys.

Lake lets out a sigh, then whispers, "Talk to me."

"Just flashbacks about Jen," Mason's voice rumbles low.

Realization creeps into the back of my mind. I knew Mason's sister died in an accident. I was thirteen back then and still trying to adjust to the new wealthy lifestyle after my dad made it big. I didn't know much about Mason, Lake, and Falcon. It was during my senior year that I learned as much as I could about the wealthy society I was apart of, so I would fit in easier once I started at the Academy.

Come to think of it, I'm only a year older now than Mason was when he lost his sister.

"Nothing to worry about," Mason breathes, but the words sound heavy with grief.

"What triggered it?" Lake asks.

Mason remains quiet for a while.

My eyes widen when my nose starts to itch.

Crap, don't sneeze.

I wiggle my nose and moving as quietly as I can, I rub it.

"The girls," Mason whispers. "Certain things they do remind me of Jen." He pauses for a couple of seconds, then adds, "Then there was the avalanche, and not being able to hold onto Kingsley."

The rhythm of my heart slows down as if it's trying to whisper the beats so the guys won't hear.

"You don't want to take the meds? It will help with the shock."

Lying in the darkness and listening to them whisper, slowly begins to alter my perception of Mason.

"I'm not going to take that shit. I'll deal with the flashes."

"Don't take it out on Kingsley, though," Lake murmurs.

There's another moment of silence, and I find I'm holding my breath, so I won't miss what Mason says next.

"It hurts to be around her." His admission makes me press my lips together, and I shut my eyes tightly, a wave of guilt hitting hard. "It's the same with Layla, but Falcon will kick my ass if I snub his girl."

"What are you going to do?" Lake asks.

"Deal with the shit somehow." Mason lets out a heavy breath. "They're not going anywhere, so I'll just have to deal."

Layla said she thought Mason's aggressive attitude was all a smokescreen. It's his way of trying to cope with his loss. I thought he hated me, but hearing he's hurting because of me... I don't know what to do with the information.

"I'm here for you," Lake mumbles, sounding half asleep.

"Thanks, buddy."

Long after they fall asleep, I lie awake, listening to the cabin creaking from the wind blowing outside.

Honestly, I'm still scared of Mason, but now that I know his offensive behavior is only a mask he hides his pain behind, I can't help but wonder if there's a way to melt the frozen shard of ice he calls a heart.

There must be something I can do to make things easier for Mason.

"Five minutes," I mumble when someone calls me.

"Kingsley!" Hearing Mason's shout has my eyes flying open as I shoot up into a sitting position. I'm disorientated and have to blink a couple of times before glancing around the dark room.

"Jen, wake up," Mason whimpers, and the heartbreaking sound instantly clears my mind of the sleep.

I glance over to where he's lying and see Lake shake Mason's shoulder. "Wake up, buddy."

Mason's breathing speeds up, and then it hitches.

I lie back down and cover my mouth with my hands as I watch Lake shift closer to Mason, wrapping his arms around him.

"I've got you," Lake whispers.

Mason's arm moves around Lake, and when he grabs hold of his shirt, my heart almost cracks in half.

Oh, my God. I've never seen anything so heartbreaking in my life.

Tears well in my eyes, and I grab hold of the covers, pressing it to my mouth.

Hearing Mason's erratic breaths only makes it so much worse.

"I'm here," Lake keeps whispering calming words.

I can only hear Mason's breaths for a while, then he gets up, and I quickly shut my eyes. I hear him walk out of the room, and when Lake doesn't follow him, I assume he went back to sleep.

I sit up, and worried about Mason, I throw the covers back and scoot to the foot of the bed. I use the wall to help me get up, then peek out onto the landing, but I can't see him.

Knowing I'll wake everyone if I hop, I carefully put pressure on my right foot. The pain is sharp, and I cringe through it as I take an unsteady step. I only manage to get to the banister at the top of the stairs and glancing down, I see Mason below.

His hands are linked at the back of his neck as he paces up and down the length of the living room. Suddenly, he picks up his phone from the coffee table and does something on it before he walks toward the stairs.

Oh, crap.

Panicking that I'll be caught red-handed, I use the banister so I can quickly move into the corner. I hunch down and pulling a worried face, I say a quick prayer he won't see me.

Mason walks back into the room and gets something. Coming out of the room again, he stops right by the stairs.

Shit.

"Don't wake them," he whispers.

Slowly, I pull myself up and look at him.

He doesn't turn his head my way and begins to go down the stairs.

I watch him shrug on his jacket. He pockets his phone and wallet, then walks to the front door. He pulls it open and stepping outside, he looks up to me. It's the first time I don't see any hostility on his face.

Just the sadness.

Mason, unmasked.

The beauty of a fallen angel… with broken wings.

When he starts to pull the door closed, I want to call out for him to wait. I want to ask him where he's going.

He pauses, and as if he can hear my thoughts, he murmurs, "I'm going home, so don't worry. Don't wake the others."

I nod and quickly ask, "How will you get home?"

"I called a cab."

"Have a safe trip and text Lake or Falcon once you get home."

Pain tightens his features right before he turns away and closes the door behind him.

"What was Jennifer like?" I ask while we're driving back to the Academy.

With me almost spraining half my body and Mason leaving yesterday morning, we all decided to pack up and head home.

"She was always positive," Lake answers.

Without taking his eyes from the road, Falcon adds, "She had an infectious laughter."

Lake glances over his shoulder at me. "They were really close."

Not wanting to cause Mason more pain, I ask, "What can I do so I don't remind him of her?"

"What do you mean?" In the rearview mirror, I see a frown forming on Falcon's face.

"Ahh fuck," Lake mutters. "You weren't sleeping?"

"No, sorry." I feel shitty for eavesdropping, but I'm glad I overheard them. At least, I can try to help and not make things worse.

"I'm still lost here," Falcon calls out.

It wakes Layla, who's been sleeping most of the journey, and lifting her head, she squints at the road. "How can you be lost? We're on the right road," she mumbles, then leans her head back down.

I let out a bark of laughter that has Lake chuckling.

After the short interruption, Lake answers my question from before, "Just be yourself, Kingsley."

I sigh, wondering if that's the best thing to do.

Lake adds, "And don't worry about it. You'll see, he'll be back to normal when we get to the Academy."

Normal?

Is the aggressive version really the normal Mason?

"What was Mason like before the accident?" I ask.

48

Lake yawns and mumbles, "Not so stubborn. Less rough around the edges."

Lake drifts off to sleep, and I lean my head against the window as I stare at Layla's hair that's sticking up from the front passenger seat.

I'm going to take a page out of Layla's book.

Kill him with kindness.

Okay, maybe not the killing part... yet.

Chapter 5

Mason

The Academy is like a ghost town, and it's just what I needed. I texted Falcon and Lake yesterday when I got back, letting them know I'm fine.

I've spent all my time in the suite, pushing every one of my ghosts back into the vault deep inside my heart, and ignoring life by watching all the YouTube videos I can find about the current most expensive supercars.

Lying on the couch in just my boxers, I begin to drift off when I hear a thud against the door. Frowning, I sit up, and when I hear a shuffle, I walk closer.

Falcon and Lake won't be back this soon, will they?

I'm just about to reach for the door when it opens, and a mess of dark hair slams into my chest.

"Dafuuuc?" I grumble as I scowl down at the rat's nest planted against me.

"Crap, sorry."

Fucking Kingsley.

My eyebrow darts up when she places her left hand on my abs and pushes herself back.

Getting a view of her face, I watch her blink while she stares at my chest. She pulls an exaggerated impressed face, then nods. "Not bad, Mason."

"You've seen it before," I growl. "What the hell are you doing here?"

"Oh," she grins up at me as if we're best friends. "We decided to come home early."

The rest of the gang comes down the hallway and stops behind Kingsley, their arms full of baggage.

Falcon's eyes sweep over me, and grinning, he says, "Haven't seen those boxers in a while."

"It won't suck itself," Kingsley reads the writing plastered over my fucking dick, then she lets out a bark of laughter and almost loses her damn balance.

"Fuck off," I snap, and turning around, I stalk to my room. Grabbing the sweatpants draped over the side of my bed, I quickly pull them on, then walk back out to get my phone.

"Every muscle in my body aches," Layla groans.

Wagging his eyebrows, Falcon offers, "I can massage *every* muscle for you."

51

"Yeah?" she teases him, her voice dropping to a seductive tone.

"I need a shower," Kingsley mutters from where she's planted herself on the couch, right next to my phone. She's leaning back, and her eyes are closed.

"Won't argue with you there," I mumble as I walk closer and swipe my phone from the couch. "It looks like something exploded in your hair."

She sits up and pats her hand over the wild mess as if it will help. "Ugh, I didn't have time to straighten it before we left."

I let out a chuckle, "So this is you, all-natural?" I glance over her, and even though she looks just fine, I can't help but take advantage of the opportunity. "You must spend quite some time getting ready every morning."

She swings her eyes to me and giving me a your-opinion-doesn't-matter-look, she says, "Lucky for me, I don't give a flying fuck about what you think of my looks."

And just like that everything is back to normal between Kingsley and me.

I was a little worried she would be weird around me after she caught me sneaking out of the cabin.

Kingsley's phone begins to ring, and her ringtone almost makes me grin. It has Lake and Falcon chuckling.

'It's your daddy calling, and you know he's gonna chew your ear off. It's your daddy calling, all you're gonna hear is blah, blah, blah, blah, blah.'

"Hey, Dad," she answers. "No, we came back early." She smiles. "Yeah, it was okay."

She leans back against the couch and catches me watching her.

I glance away as she continues, "No, nothing happened. We just felt like coming back before the other students." After a short silence, she quickly rambles, "Someone's knocking at the door. Gotta go. Love you, Dad." She hangs up and pulls a worried face at the phone. "That was close."

"You're not telling your father about the avalanche?" I ask.

"There's no need to worry him about something that's done and dealt with," she brushes it off.

Changing the subject, Layla asks, "Which ringtone do you have for me?"

"Oh!" Instantly the frown vanishes, and Kingsley grins at Layla. "You're going to love it."

A moment later *'You are my sunshine,'* comes from the phone.

"Aww… thanks, my friend," Layla coos.

Lake leans over the back of the chair. "And me?"

Kingsley looks at him from over her shoulder. "Have you heard of Lucas, the spider?"

"Yeah."

"You have Lucas." Kingsley presses play, and then you hear, *'What you eating? I'm starving.'*

"That's perfect," Falcon chuckles. "Now, I have to hear mine."

"One sec." Kingsley scrolls to his name, and then I let out a bark of laughter. *"You have a call from God. Haa-llelujah! Haa-llelujah!"*

"Badass," Falcon grins, obviously happy with it.

"This is Mason's." Kingsley grins mischievously, which tells me I'm not going to like it. Then a butler's serious voice sounds up, *'Excuse me, but I'm afraid someone is endeavoring to contact you telephonically. Shall I tell them to fuck off?'*

Lake cracks up, disappearing behind the couch, which doesn't help shit, seeing as I can hear the fucker laughing his ass off.

Two weeks later, things have kind of returned to normal, and it's helped silence the memories.

I glare at the tie. "Fuck it," I mutter as I toss it back on the bed. People should be glad I'm wearing a damn suit.

Grabbing a pair of cufflinks and my watch, I walk out into the living room. Sitting down on the couch, I quickly put on the cufflinks.

Taking hold of the *Cartier* watch I got from Jennifer, I stare down at it.

That was our last Christmas together.

Letting out a sigh, I strap it onto my wrist before getting back up.

Lake comes out of his room, fumbling with his tie. "I still can't make one," he complains.

I walk over, and taking hold of the tie, I fix it for him.

"Aww… you make such a cute couple," Layla teases.

I glance over my shoulder and see her and Kingsley come in.

When I spot the keycard in her hand, I frown. "You have a keycard now?"

"Just borrowed it from Falcon," she says.

I think it's time we each move into our own suite.

I finish making Lake's tie, then pat him on the chest. "See you at the chamber of torture."

Every year the Christmas Eve party is held at the main offices of CRC.

"Hold up, let's leave together," Falcon says.

When Falcon takes his keys from his pocket, Lake protests, "No, put those away. We're all going in the Bentley."

"Why?" I frown, not liking the sound of that at all.

"Because you fuckers left me with that viper last time. If we go in the Bentley, there's no space for her."

Shaking my head, I walk out of the suite first. As I press the button for the elevator, I smell something sweet and glancing to my side, I see that it's Kingsley.

She's busy checking something in her purse. Her hair is styled in soft curls. She glances up, and her blue eyes lock on mine.

I might not get along with her, but even I have to admit she looks beautiful in the black dress she's wearing.

Turning my eyes away from her, I glance up at the numbers, and as soon as the elevator opens, I step inside.

Kingsley walks in and then stops the doors from closing as the rest of the gang approaches us.

I step back and lean against the wall, and when Kingsley bumps into my left arm, I flick a glare her way. She quickly moves to the corner and smiles at Lake when he goes to stand by her.

After Falcon and Layla get in, he leans down and whispers in her ear, "You look beautiful, my rainbow."

Having seen enough, I turn my head only to lock eyes with Kingsley again. Her head is tilted to the side, a far-off expression on her face.

"You planning my death, Hunt?" I ask when she still staring at me as the doors open on the ground floor.

She blinks a couple of times, then grunts, "Huh?"

"I asked," I say a little louder, "are you planning my death?"

She lifts her chin, and walking out of the elevator, she says, "No need to. I planned that shit a long time ago."

That mouth of hers…

When we walk out of The Hope Diamond, Lake lets out a groan when he sees Serena, and urgently whispers, "Get your assess to the Bentley!"

"Who am I riding with?" Serena asks.

Lake walks so damn fast to where the Bentley is parked, with Kingsley and Layla right behind him, you'd swear they were having a competition to see who can get away from Serena the quickest.

My eyes snap to Serena, and I take a couple of steps closer to her. "I didn't know you liked to bake."

She gives me a vexed look. "What on earth are you talking about?"

"The pie you gave Layla just before she was rushed to ICU." I keep my face blank even though anger is quickly filling my chest.

"I don't have time for this, Mason," she snaps.

When she takes a step toward Falcon, who's watching us from where he's standing a couple of feet behind me, I grab hold of her arm.

Her eyes flick to me. "Let go of me this instant."

I close the distance between us and leaning down, I whisper, "I know what you did."

Pulling back, our eyes lock, and I see the manic rage burn in hers.

"Falcon," she calls out, "are you going to allow your friend to treat me this way?"

I glance over my shoulder. "Wait at the car for me."

Falcon nods and walks over to where everyone is standing, watching us with worried expressions.

"Just because you're the future President of CRC, it gives you no right to treat me this way," Serena spits at me.

Letting go of her arm, I take a step back and let my eyes go over her. "Where are you going?"

"The Christmas Eve function, of course. Mrs. Reyes invited me."

A slow smile forms on my face. "Ahh... I see." I let out a breath and shaking my head, I give her a look of pity. "I hate to break this to you, but as the future President of CRC, you're officially banned from attending any function held by my company."

Even with all the makeup on, her cheeks turn red.

"See what I did there?" I ask as I sneer down at her, and I snap my fingers in front of her face. "That's all it takes, Serena, and you're cut off." A smile splits over my face again as I begin to walk away from her. "If I were you, I'd start worrying about my next move."

"Why, Mason?" she yells.

The shrillness of her voice tells me I've succeeded in scaring her.

"Because you fucked with my friend."

Chapter 6

Kingsley

Sitting in the back of the car with Layla and Falcon, I keep staring at the side profile of Mason's face.

He doesn't look upset after his argument with Serena, and wondering what it was about, I ask, "What did Serena do?"

When Mason and Lake keep quiet, Falcon says, "It's just time we severed ties with her."

I lean forward so I can see Falcon because Layla is sitting between us. "Not that I'm best friends with her, but should I distance myself from her, as well?"

"Hunt," Mason says, and my eyes dart to him. He doesn't look up from his phone, as he continues, "You have a choice. Serena or Layla."

"What?" Layla gasps. "You don't get to decide who can be friends with me."

Hurt by his words, I sit back and stare out the window.

So, I'm only here because of my friendship with Layla.
Well, that sucks.

"At least, now I know where I stand," I mumble. "So much for thinking I was a part of the group and not just Layla's sidekick."

"Of course you're part of the group," Layla says, and taking hold of my hand, she squeezes it.

I give her a thankful smile and decide to let it go seeing as it was Mason, and seriously, does it even matter what he thinks?

When we reach CRC, and Lake parks the car, I open the door and climb out. My ankle has pretty much healed, but I'm still careful with every step I take, so I don't go and sprain it again.

Walking toward the entrance, Lake falls in next to me and holds his arm for me to take.

"It's healed," I remind him.

He smiles warmly at me, "I know, but let me be a gentleman."

I grin at him as I take his arm and give it a quick hug. "You're special people, Lake Cutler."

"Yeah, with the patience of a Saint seeing as he has to deal with you," Mason mumbles as he walks past us.

I glare at him as he tucks his phone into the inside pocket of his suit jacket.

"Aww… Mason, cute as always." I roll my eyes at him, even though he can't see.

His voice rumbles as he walks into the building, "Always a pleasure, babe."

"Asshole," I grumble after him.

A damn hot asshole in the suit he's wearing, but an asshole nonetheless.

"This is nothing like the Thanksgiving function," Layla whispers, where we're standing to the side.

I lean closer to her and whisper back, "Yeah, I know what you mean. It feels more intimidating with just the families."

"Right? Talking about intimidating," she mutters as Mrs. Reyes comes toward us.

Mrs. Reyes holds a wine glass in her hand, her pinky sticking in the air all dainty like. There's a disgusted look on her face as if she just stepped in crap with her satin pumps from Prada.

"Miss Shepard," she pauses and lets her eyes slowly sweep over Layla, "you're here."

Woo-oowwww!

"Mrs. Reyes," Layla inclines her head as if she's greeting royalty, "I hope you've been well."

Mrs. Reyes' eyes crawl over to me, and I actually have an eye-spasm when I fight the urge to roll my eyes at her snootiness.

"You brought a friend," she sneers condescendingly.

Fight it, Kingsley.

You can beat the urge of the eye roll.

"Kingsley, this is Falcon's mother, Clare Reyes," Layla introduces us.

Yeah, and now I'm just plain stuck.

How do I greet this woman?

Can't say it's a pleasure…

I'd say you're a cow, but that would be an insult to all the cows out there…

I have to suppress the grin brought on from the last thought, and instead, I just nod at her. It's better for everyone here if I keep my mouth shut right now.

"From which family?" she demands.

"Hunt." I let a wide smile spread over my face. "Doctor Stephen Hunt is my father. You might have met him already? He's a plastic surgeon."

Mrs. Reyes' eyes narrow on me, which means she got the insult I subtly threw her way.

"The name is unfamiliar," she sneers. "But it's to be expected, seeing as you're a friend of Miss Shepard."

Falcon and Mason come up behind her. They must've heard what we were talking about because Mason throws his arm around Mrs. Reyes shoulders, and smiling at her, he says, "Don't be so vain, Clare. No one will judge you for having some work done."

Dude… bravo!

I want to high-five him, but instead, I settle for grinning at him.

When Mason actually smiles at Layla and me, my eyes widen, and I stare at him with surprise.

He should definitely smile more. It transforms him from beast to beauty… one hell of a sexy and fu –

My thoughts screech to a halt when he winks at me.

I start to blink as if I'm malfunctioning, which has him chuckling as he steers Mrs. Reyes away from us.

"Mason, how dare you!" she snaps at him, trying to shake his arm from her shoulders.

Mason tightens his hold around her, and with authority lacing his words, he says, "Seeing as I'll be taking over the finances soon, let's talk about how much you spend on your face every year."

"Did he just wink at you?" Layla asks, sounding as surprised as me, then she takes a sip of her soda.

"Probably got an eye spasm," I mumble. "It could be an allergic reaction to Mrs. Reyes, seeing as I had the same problem."

Layla snorts when she tries to keep from laughing out loud and quickly covers her face. She rushes from the room, and I set after her, laughter bursting from me because she just snorted her soda.

I haven't formally met Falcon, Mason, and Lake's parents. Well, with the exception of Mrs. Reyes. So, when Mr. Reyes announces it's time for dinner, I feel all kinds of uncomfortable. I follow Layla to the dining room, aka the ballroom, which has a table big enough to seat half the students at Trinity.

Oh. Fun.

Julian takes a seat at the head of the table, with Mr. Reyes at the foot. For a moment, I forget myself, and I pull a this-isn't-weird-at-all-face as I watch the older generation split from the younger.

"Everything alright, Miss Hunt?" Mr. Reyes asks, catching me red-handed.

Shoot.

"Oh yes, just a cramp in my foot. I recently sprained it," I lie through my teeth. "Thank you for asking, though."

"Good. Good," he murmurs.

Mason sits on Julian's right with Lake next to him. Falcon takes Julian's left side, but he first pulls out Layla's chair for her, which is next to his.

I'm glad my friend found such a caring guy. I sit down next to Layla and glancing up, I catch Mason looking at me.

I smile brightly at him, which instantly makes him frown.

I need to start keeping score of all my wins.

When everyone is seated, Julian rises to his feet, and holding a flute in his hand, he says, "This is a first for me. I'll appreciate your understanding if I fumble a bit."

My impression of Julian is the same as the night of the Thanksgiving event, he comes across as the perfect businessman. His behavior is professional, his eyes are sharp, and the invisible wall he has around him will knock you flat on your ass if you try to get close to him.

Almost like Mason, who's just missing the professionalism because he's too busy being a jerk.

"It's been quite the year," Julian begins his toast. He smiles down at Falcon with affection, and it makes my heart go aww. "Falcon has met this lovely woman," he looks to Layla, "Thank you for joining us."

Layla gives him a grateful look, "Thank you for having me."

Julian glances over the table, then he frowns. "Where's Stephanie?"

"Oh, she's just taking a call. She'll join us soon. Do carry on," Mr. Reyes answers.

"Give me a moment. I need to check my notes," he chuckles, making his half of the table chuckle.

He quickly scans over the card next to his silverware, then continues, "Mason," Julian locks eyes with Mason, and it feels as if there's a lot being said between them with just one glance. "I'm looking forward to working with you. I would like to believe Jennifer would've been happy for us."

My eyes widen at his words, then they jump to Mason's face, and seeing the flash of pain, I turn my head and look at Mr. and Mrs. Chargill.

Mr. Chargill stares at the table cloth, while Mrs, Chargill downs her glass of wine.

I have to wonder if Julian's really oblivious to the wave of heartache his statement caused.

He's just about to continue when Stephanie comes into the room. She hurries over to Mr. Reyes and whispers something near his ear.

Mr. Reyes gets up, then glances around the table. "Please continue with dinner. We'll only be a minute." He gestures to where Stephanie is waiting by the door. "Julian, join us."

The older generation murmurs amongst themselves, then Mrs. Reyes snaps her fingers in the air, making staff stream into the room with plates of food.

"We might as well eat. No use in letting Stephanie spoil dinner."

My jaw drops, and under the table, I pat Layla's leg.

"Have another glass of wine, Clare," Mason's mom expresses with annoyance. "You're going to give me indigestion."

Good for Mrs. Chargill for speaking up, and I now see where Mason inherited his knack for sarcasm.

Mrs. Reyes leans forward and glares at Mrs. Chargill. "If there's any left after you're done with it."

Mrs. Cutler lets out a sigh, "Thank you for that, ladies. You've just added a wrinkle to my forehead with your bickering."

I hunch over and duck my head, pressing my lips together. Squeezing my eyes shut, I try not to laugh, but a snort escapes. My hands shoot to my face, and I try to hide behind it.

"You're going to burst a vein, Hunt," Mason states wryly. "No one will blame you for laughing at our dinner drama."

"Candice," Mrs. Reyes scowls down the length of the table at Mason. "Maybe if you indulged less, you would have more time to reign in your son?"

Ouch. Low blow, Lady. Low blow.

"Oh, for god's sake, Clare," Mrs. Chargill snaps. "Drop your holier than thou attitude. It makes you look like you're constipated."

I glance at Mason, and seeing his mouth lift at the corner makes me feel better about wanting to crack up.

"Who said family gatherings were boring?" Mr. Cutler mumbles. He looks down at his food, then calls out, "Son, bring your plate."

Lake gets up and carries his plate over to where his dad is, and I watch as Mr. Cutler swaps some of his food for Lake's.

"There's one more, Dad," Lake says, pointing to a piece of liver.

"I need new glasses. Darling, remind me to go for a check-up," he mutters to Mrs. Cutler.

When Lake comes back to his seat and sits down, he sees me staring. "I don't eat livers, and my dad gets heartburn from the sauce."

"Oh, I forgot again," Mrs. Reyes says way too nicely, which tells me she knows but didn't care.

Smiling, I whisper, "I think it's sweet of you to swap out what you don't like."

"Hunt, you think everything Lake does is sweet. You do know he's engaged, right?"

Turning my face away from the parents, I take a page out of Falcon's book, as I use my middle finger to wipe an invisible tear from under my eye.

Mason grins, "Such a lady."

"I'd get up and curtsy, but that would totally ruin your impression of me."

He lets out a bark of laughter, which startles the parents. I quickly glance at them, and when I see Mr. Chargill staring at Mason with a look of awe on his face, it makes a wave of emotion crash over me.

When was the last time he heard his son laugh?

Chapter 7

Mason

I'm not going to lie, Layla and Kingsley totally made the evening more fun than it normally is.

When we get back to the campus, Lake stops in front of the dorms for us to get out before he goes to park the car.

"The girls are out cold," Falcon says from the back. "Mason, can you carry Kingsley?"

As I open my door, Lake grabs hold of my arm, "Don't throw her in the pool or do something stupid just because she's sleeping," he warns.

"I wasn't even thinking about it, but now that you mentioned it..." I joke as I wag my eyebrows while getting out.

"You're making me old before my time," Lake grumbles.

Walking to Kingsley's side, I open the door, and slipping my arms under her, I lift her to my chest.

She lets out a groan when Lake shuts the door for me. He quickly hushes her, "Shh… go back to sleep."

Kingsley's hand pats against my chest, and she mumbles, "'Kay." And then she snuggles her face into my shoulder, stunning the hell out of me. There's an unexpected burst of tenderness in my chest, and I try to ignore it as I begin to walk with her.

Lake jogs past me so he can open the door to Layla's suite, then he heads back to the car to park it. I follow Falcon into Layla's bedroom and wait for him to first lay her down before I walk to the other side of the bed with Kingsley in my arms.

My first instinct is to just drop her on the bed, but then I glance down and see her face. Holding her in my arms, with her face so close to mine, makes the tender feeling from before come rushing back.

"Mason," Falcon whispers. My eyes dart to him, and he indicates for me to put her down.

Bending over, I place her on the bed, and before I can pull back, she lifts her head and presses a kiss to my jaw, then sleepily whispers, "Night."

My fucking heart all but stops as I turn my head and stare at her, shocked out of my mind.

What the fuck just happened?

"Mason," Falcon whispers again, yanking me out of the stupor.

I quickly pull back and walk right out of the room. I keep going until I reach our suite and go to stand in front of the windows.

Why am I breathing so fast?

'Cause you rushed back to the suite. It's not because she kissed you.

"What's wrong with Mason?" Lake asks behind me. "He looks like he's seen a ghost."

"Nope, worse," Falcon chuckles.

Lake comes to stand next to me and stares at my face, "What's worse?"

I shake my head and growl, "Kingsley kissed me."

"Say again?" Lake leans forward, trying to catch my eyes.

I give him a disgruntled look. "Hunt's lips touched my face."

He quickly pulls back while pressing his lips together.

"If you laugh, I'm going to beat the shit out of you," I warn him.

Lake darts away from me as laughter explodes from him. I turn and begin to stalk after him, but the fucker ducks behind Falcon, who's pulling a face as if it's actually killing him to not laugh.

"I get jumped by a sleeping madwoman, and you're both laughing your asses off. I see how it is."

I struggle to keep a straight face as Lake slides to the floor, holding onto Falcon's leg while he almost pisses himself cracking up.

Falcon has to brace his hands on his knees, so he doesn't go down, his shoulders shaking.

Giving up, I smile because even though they're laughing at my expense, there's nothing as good in the world as seeing my friends happy.

Laying in bed, with my hands tucked behind my head, I stare up at the dark ceiling.

Lake's out in the living room, and for what has to be the hundredth time, he begins to whistle the fucking wedding march.

"Lake!" I shout.

It's silent for a couple of seconds, then the fucker starts again. I let out a growl as I throw the covers back, and grabbing my pillow, I dart out of bed. Yanking my door open, I run to where Lake's lying on the couch, and it has the fucker squeaking like a girl. "Shit!" He shoots up and over the back of the couch.

When I catch up to him, he sinks to the floor, and I smack the shit out of him with the pillow.

"Ah-hh-hh-hh!" he yells while laughing at the same time.

"You're seriously having a pillow fight?" Falcon asks from where he's leaning against the door jamb of his bedroom.

"No," Lake wheezes through the laughter, "save me."

"From what?" I ask. "It's a goose down pillow. The shit is softer than a newborn baby's ass."

"Soft like Kingsley's lips?" Lake asks as he crawls away.

I throw the pillow against his back.

"Lake," Falcon says, his voice surprisingly serious, "give Mason a break."

Lake gets up, nodding as if his father just scolded him. He even has the fucking innocent look plastered over his face.

Falcon continues with the same serious tone, "He hasn't been with a woman in… what? Three months?"

Lake's face begins to turn red from keeping in his laugher as he keeps nodding. "It's a new record. I can understand why he's shocked by a kiss."

I walk up to Lake and slap him upside the head before I make my way to Falcon, but the fucker darts back into his room and slams the door shut.

Behind me, Lake begins to whistle the fucking tune again, and as I turn around to him, he runs for his room. A second later, the door slams shut behind his ass.

"That's it. I'm getting my own place," I yell, and walking over to my pillow, I pick it up.

"You love me too much," Lake yells from behind the safety of his door.

"You can't live without us," Falcon joins in.

"Fuckers," I grumble with a wide smile on my face.

But they're both right. I love them, and I can't live without them.

Classes have started again and sitting in the restaurant, I watch Lake gorge down a bigass lobster.

"You know Lobsters are arthropods, right?"

Lake swallows the bite he took, and cracking the lobster's shell open, says, "Don't care."

Pulling up an image of arthropods on my phone, I hold it up to Lake while pointing at the screen. "Lobster equals this shit."

Lake's eyes dart up, and when he focuses on the picture, he drops the tail. "Aww... fuck. You just killed lobster for me."

I grin at him. "Revenge for last night." Having succeeded in my mission, I get up and walk away while whistling the wedding march that's been stuck in my fucking head all morning.

"Who's getting married?" Serena asks, gathering her books while getting up from a nearby table.

Not being able to resist the opportunity, I taunt her, "Not you, that's for sure."

West comes to stand behind Serena and fuck, it actually turns my stomach seeing the two leeches together.

"You know who else isn't getting married?" West asks.

Don't fucking go there.

Our eyes lock, and the hatred I feel for the fucker rushes through my body. I close my hands into tight fists at my sides, so I don't fucking kill him right here.

West walks closer, stupidly putting himself between me and the exit. He begins to grin, and the students must feel the tension because they clear the area around us.

The fucker must have a thing for pain. He's much shorter than me and has never won a fight between us, yet the idiot keeps coming back.

"Just leave, West," Lake says as he comes to stand next to me.

"Why?" West gives Lake a smug look that has me narrowing my eyes. When the fucker takes a step closer to Lake and then dares to shove his finger at Lake's chest, rage explodes behind my eyes.

"You're no –" He doesn't get to finish the sentence as I grab hold of his shirt and yank him away from Lake, and out of the restaurant. The second we're outside, my fist connects with his jaw. I feel the hedonistic satisfaction, I can only get from beating the life out of this piece of shit, begin to course through my veins.

"Don't ever fucking touch Lake," I growl as I repeatedly slam my fist into his face.

I pull my arm back, but then West chuckles while he brings a hand to his nose. Wiping his fingers through the blood, he chuckles again, but the sound is hollow and bleak.

"There must've been a lot of blood when the branch skewered your arm to her." A guilt-ridden expression flashes over his face before it's replaced by the usual look of smugness.

My entire body begins to shake as haunting memories of that night flood me all at once.

Her cheek is resting on the branch as if she just leaned forward and decided to fall asleep.

Blood trickles from her mouth, and I hear the gurgling sound again.

"Jen!"

I'm stopped by the branch pinning me to her chest.

She gasps for air.

"Jennifer!"

Chapter 8

Kingsley

"Layla!" I point a finger to where Mason is punching the shit out of West.

"Crap, I'll go get Falcon," she says and then runs toward the dorms.

I jog closer to the fight, not having any idea of what to do.

"There must've been a lot of blood when the branch skewered your arm to her."

The words shudder through me and fill me with shock, bringing me to a stop slightly to the right side of West.

My eyes dart to Mason, and his face is set in hard lines, his body shaking, and it's then I realize what Mason looks like when he's angry.

He looks like thunder.

"I'm going to kill you," Mason growls, and I let out a shriek when his fist connects with West's face.

Lake tries to intervene, but Mason glares at him like a raging maniac, "Stay the fuck back!"

This is bad.

I glance over my shoulder to see if Falcon is coming, and when there's no sight of him, I tighten my hands at my sides, anxiety making me feel jittery.

"You don't get to talk about my sister." Mason's breaths become harsh gasps, and he doesn't stop punching West.

Falcon suddenly runs up to the fight, and he darts between them. He shoves West hard, and my eyes only have time to widen before West crashes into me.

I go down with a shriek as West falls over me, and something hard connects with my mouth. I freeze from the jolting pain, shutting my eyes tightly.

When a copper taste fills my mouth, I shove West off of me and dart up. I spit and almost gag. "Eww… I got his blood in my mouth."

Layla rushes to me, and using the sleeve of her sweater, she wipes over my mouth, but it has me flinching away.

"Crap, Kingsley," she gasps. "It's your own blood."

"It is?" I frown and brushing my thumb over my lip, I flinch again. "Ugh, it is."

"Are you okay?" Lake asks as he places a hand on my shoulder, leaning a little down to see my face.

"I'm okay." I feel blood dribble down to my chin, and quickly cover my mouth so I won't bleed all over the place. "I'm going to clean up," I mumble behind my hand and begin to walk toward my dorm.

Seconds later, I hear Layla say, "I'll take care of her."

Glancing over my shoulder, I see Mason stalking after me. He catches up and darts in front of me. Grabbing my shoulders, he snaps, "Let me see."

"It's nothing," I argue, not moving my hand.

I swear I hear him growl, and he grabs hold of my wrist, yanking my hand away. His eyes land sharply on the cut, and when the blood trickles all the way to the bottom of my chin, he reaches up with his other hand and wipes the blood away. He rubs it off on his jacket, which makes my eyes bulge with surprise, and without another word, he grabs my wrist and begins to drag me toward The Hope Diamond.

"I'm okay." I pull back against his hold, but Mason just ignores me and hauls me all the way to the elevator.

A drop of blood splats on the clean floor, and I quickly cover my chin and bottom lip with my free hand, so I don't end up leaving a trail.

Mason presses the button, still not letting go of my wrist, and when the doors ping open, he yanks me inside. I catch myself from stumbling into him.

Mason leans past me and presses the number for the top floor, and pulling back, his eyes land on my face. He finally lets go of my wrist and shrugs out of his jacket. Shoving my hand away, he almost freaking smothers me when he presses his jacket to my mouth.

Glaring at him, I mumble, "Can't breathe."

"Just hold the fucking thing there," he snaps angrily.

I take hold of it, moving it a little down.

The doors open, and Mason grabs my left arm, dragging me again.

"Hey!" I snap, but the stupid jacket muffles the sound.

He doesn't stop once he's inside, but instead, stalks toward a bedroom, and right through it to the bathroom. My eyes dart curiously around the room, and I notice the place is pristine, unlike my own.

In the bathroom, Mason lets go of my arm, then takes hold of my hips, and when he lifts me, I let out a squeak. He sets me down on the counter next to the sink, and leaning into the shower, he grabs a face cloth. While wetting the fabric, he washes his hands before he impatiently shoves my legs open so he can step into the open space.

Ahhhh… My brain hums with surprise, unable to think of a suitable reaction. All I can do is blink from all the manhandling.

Mason begins to dab at the cut, and I flinch back from the sting. "Dude… it hurts."

He takes hold of my chin and keeping me still, continues to dab at the cut, but at least it's gentler this time. He cleans the blood from my chin, then reaches up to the cabinet against the wall, totally leaning into me.

With the extreme close up view of his chest, all I can do is stare like an idiot. His spicy scent wafts up my nose, and it makes me lose my mind for a moment.

"Love the aftershave."

Mason pulls back and sets a small first aid kit down next to me. His head is bowed as he looks for whatever he needs, and my eyes glide over the sharp lines of his jaw, that's covered in a light dusting of stubble.

"Are you taking a break from shaving?" I ask.

"Shut up, Hunt," he growls low.

He takes out an alcohol swab and brings it to my face.

I yank back. "It stings."

His left-hand shoots behind my neck, and with a tight grip, he forces me to keep still.

As he begins to clean the cut, my eyes start to water from the sharp smell. It burns the cut, making a whimper slip from me.

"Almost done," he whispers, his tone much softer.

He drops the swab in the sink and tilting his head, he leans even closer to me, as he looks at the cut. I feel his breath fan over my neck and freeze as a wave of awareness wells up in me.

"It doesn't look like you need stitches," he says, totally oblivious to my reaction of having him so close to me.

When he moves back a couple of inches, and his eyes meet mine, I quickly glance to the side.

"Relax, Hunt."

Dude, you're all up in my personal space. I get a front-row view of your jaw, your mouth, your... everything. Oh, and you smell sooooo good.

Yep. No way I'm going to relax.

He squirts some ointment onto his finger, then takes hold of my chin as he dabs it over the cut.

I glance away again, so I don't keep staring at his face, and my eyes land on a scar on his left arm, stretching from above his wrist and all the way to his elbow.

Not thinking, I lift my hand and brush a finger along the length of the scar.

Mason freezes, and when I feel his eyes burn on me, I drop my hand quickly.

"You better not be pitying me right now," he warns.

"Just a moment of insanity brought on by the fumes of all the crap you're shoving in my face," I quickly defend my stupid action.

He sticks a butterfly bandage over the cut, then he brings his eyes back to mine as he places his hands on the counter on either side of me.

Uhmmm....

I stare back, having no idea what to do right now.

"Thank you," I whisper, thinking that's what he's waiting for.

His eyes are still smoldering with anger from the fight with West, and I'm about to start squirming when he says with a low rumble, "I'm sorry you got hurt."

My eyebrow shoots sky-high because I've never heard this man use the words 'I'm sorry' before.

He pulls back. "Don't give me that look, Hunt. You're going to make me regret apologizing."

I point to my face. "You mean this look of total disbelief?"

"Kingsley!"

"Ma-aason." I widen my eyes, and when a smile starts to pull at my lips, I cringe from the sting.

"Serves you right," he mumbles as he begins to clear the mess from the sink.

Maybe I have a temporary concussion because I hop off the counter and pat him on the arm. "Thanks for fixing me up, but seriously, it's a good thing for all of mankind you didn't go into the medical field. You have zero bedside manners."

Mason swings around, drops the cloth back in the sink, and then he's crowding my personal space.

He leans even closer, and I swallow hard when I feel his breath fan over the side of my face. "You wouldn't be able to handle my bedside manners, Hunt."

Don't argue. Let him win this round.

Don't!

"Is that a dare?" I whisper back.

Oh, woman. Why? Why do you have to have the last word?

He pulls slightly back, his eyes locking with mine. I resist the urge to swallow hard. This time he stares at me until I feel thoroughly out of my depth because deep down, I know he's too much for me to handle.

He's too hot, too intense, and so much stronger than me. With the emphasis on the hot part right now.

His eyes slowly drift down to my mouth, and I almost lick my lips, but luckily, I still have some common sense left, and remember the cut.

"You're quick with that mouth of yours, but the way your eyes dilated and your breaths sped up, tells me you're all talk and no action," he murmurs.

The sound of a door slamming shatters the moment, and then I hear Layla call, "Kingsley, are you here?"

I pull away from Mason and rush out of the bathroom to where Layla is standing in the living room.

"All patched up," I say sounding a little breathless and taking her hand, I drag her out of the suite as fast as I possibly can.

"Are you okay?" she asks when we get to the elevator.

"Yes, and I'm starving," I use the excuse because we were on our way to get something for lunch when we came across the fight.

"Doesn't it hurt? Will you be able to eat?" she asks, her eyes scanning over my face, and I just know she can see something happened between Mason and me.

"I will suck the food through a damn straw if I have to," I say, and when the corners of her mouth tip up, I begin to ramble, "It's just weird when he's not biting my head off and doing… ahh… you know, patching up the cut."

"Yeah?" She nudges her arm against mine. "So weird, you forgot to wash your hands?"

"Shoot." I look down and then pull a grossed-out face.

"Yeah, I thought so," she chuckles, and we first stop by her room so I can clean up, before going for lunch.

Chapter 9

Mason

Standing with my hands braced on the counter, I stare at myself in the mirror.

What the hell was that?

Definitely not attraction.

She's not my type.

And she annoys me.

She might be cute and have incredible blue eyes, but that's where it ends.

And that mouth…

Which got hurt because of me.

The thought is sobering, making me remember the fight.

Hatred burns through me, turning my gaze hard. I'm going to end West. It's only a matter of time.

"Are you okay?" Falcon asks.

Turning around, I see him standing in the doorway, and I nod.

"You sure?"

"Yeah," I lie because I hate making Falcon and Lake worry.

"I'm going to ask him to leave. You guys can't keep going on like this."

"That would be for the best," Lake agrees as he leans sideways against the door jamb next to Falcon.

I shake my head. "That won't solve shit."

"Why do you want to keep him around?" Falcon asks.

"I'm not keeping him around," I answer, then my voice drops low, as I admit, "I'm torturing him."

"Yeah, the guy looks like he ran into a wall," Lake mumbles.

"You want him to live with the guilt?" Falcon asks.

The corner of my mouth twitches because I've seen small changes in him since he started dating Layla. He doesn't brush shit off anymore but digs until he gets to the truth.

"Yes." I let out a breath. "I can't carry it all by myself."

"Can we continue this conversation in the living room?" Lake asks.

"You just want to lie down," I joke as we leave my room.

"No, I just don't want to have a heart to heart with you where you shit and shower," Lake teases back. We sit down and place our feet on the table, then Lake turns all serious again. "It won't make it better."

"That's for fucking sure," I agree, then add, "Nothing can make it better. At the end of the day, she's still gone."

"Do you remember when she caught us using her nail polish to paint our cars?" Falcon asks.

A smile spreads over my face when the memory comes to me. "She was so pissed at us."

"She couldn't stay angry, though." Falcon removes his feet from the table, and resting his forearms on his thighs, he pins me with an intense look. "Jennifer loved you more than anyone. You could do anything, and she would forgive you."

"That doesn't mean I deserve forgiveness," I whisper.

"It was an accident," Lake adds.

"I had time to pull her away," I remind them.

"Did you?" Falcon asks. He gets up and comes to sit on my left side. "Did you really have time?"

I close my eyes, and the scene replays itself in my mind.

I quickly glance at Jennifer, and when her wide eyes meet mine, I feel a moment of relief.

One second.

We both look down at the branch.

Two seconds.

"Fuck that was close."

Three seconds.

"Yeah."

Four seconds.

I begin to pull my left arm back.

Five Seconds.

Squealing tires has me glancing behind us.

Six seconds.

I throw my body to the left.

Seven.

I nod with certainty. "I had seven seconds. Instead of staring at the damn branch, I should've unclipped her seatbelt. Instead of thinking about how lucky we were that it stopped inches from us, I should have pulled her to me. By the time I heard the squealing tires, Jen would have been safely in my arms."

"You had no way of knowing you'd be hit from behind," Lake argues, "Do you blame Kingsley for getting hurt?"

"What the fuck? That has nothing to do with this."

"Lake has a point," Falcon agrees.

"Do you blame yourself for her getting hurt?" Lake throws another question at me.

I scowl at him. "I blame that fucker."

"But I shoved him," Falcon says. When my eyes dart to him, our gazes lock. "So, it's actually my fault."

"Now you're getting technical," I snap.

"Exactly," Lake exclaims.

The realization of what they're trying to tell me takes the breath from my lungs. I lower my head, not able to deal with the weight of the emotions.

Lake gets up and pushing the table away, he crouches down in front of me. When I see the tears in his eyes, my heart cracks wide open.

"Please, Mace," he begs, "It's killing me watching you blame yourself." He lets out a shaky breath. "You know I'll never lie to you, right?"

I nod, unable to speak right now.

"Then, if you can't trust yourself, trust me. It was an accident. It wasn't your fault."

My body begins to shake, and my guilty conscience wars with the unbreakable bond I have with Lake.

Falcon places a hand on my back and says, "We're always the first to tell you when you fuck up, but Jen's death wasn't your fault."

It feels like world war three just exploded inside of me. I close my eyes, and my chest actually begins to ache from all the tension. I take a couple of breaths before I admit, "It's going to take a while for me to accept the fact that it was an accident."

"That's understandable," Falcon says. "We'll just keep reminding you until it's sunk in."

Lake gets up, and as he wipes his cheek, he mumbles, "Even got me crying."

"It's much more effective than the innocent look you use on us," I grumble.

"Yeah?" he lets out a burst of laughter as he moves the table back to its original place. "I'll remember that next time you threaten to beat the shit out of me."

I shake my head and grumble, "You ever use it on me again, I'll make you eat the damn pillow." I rub a hand over my chest. "Seeing you cry fucking cracked my heart open like you did with that damn lobster from this morning."

Lake sits up again and complains to Falcon, "Do you know what this ass did to me this morning?"

The elevator doors open on the top floor of CRC, and when I step out, the receptionist smiles professionally. "Good morning, Mr. Chargill."

"Morning, the President is expecting me," I say as I walk past her desk.

I knock once, and then let myself into my father's office before shutting the door behind me.

"Oh, good. You're here," my father says, getting up from behind his desk. He points to the conference desk on the right side of his office.

"Morning," I mumble as I sit down on his right.

"I want you to look at this and give me your opinion," he gets right down to business.

I glance at the screen then ask, "A proposal?"

"Yes, tell me whether it would be a loss or investment to go ahead with it."

"Okay." I pull the laptop closer and begin looking through the file.

A couple of minutes later, my father places an old folder next to me on the desk.

"What's that?"

"An old deal. When you're done with the one on the laptop, look through this one and see if you would've done anything differently."

"You're giving me homework?" I ask.

"No, I'm showing you the reality of what working here will be like."

"Did Grandpa make you do this, too?"

"No, he threw me in the deep end and told me to sink or swim." My father sits down behind his desk and returns his attention to his work.

Frowning, I turn in my seat, so I can see him. "Then why are you helping me?"

Without lifting his head, he answers, "Because I've already watched you sink once. I won't let you down a second time."

His words leave me stunned, and I can't think of a reply, so I turn back and stare at the laptop screen.

This is the first time he's spoken about anything related to Jennifer's death. I knew he was struggling with his own demons, and I never for one moment thought he let me down. I'm not as close to my parents as I used to be, but I don't blame them for it. Everyone deals differently.

Without looking at him, I ask, "Do you still sleep at the office?"

"No, your mother threatened to divorce me," he mutters.

I'm surprised it took her so long.

"Is she still drinking too much?" *Damn, I'm a shitty son.*

"No, I threatened to divorce her."

I let out a bark of laughter.

"We're going for couples counseling. You want to join us?"

This time I glance back at him from over my shoulder. "I don't need counseling." He begins to frown, and I quickly add, "I have Falcon and Lake. They're helping me deal with everything."

He nods, "That's good to hear." A couple of seconds later, he murmurs, "You should come by the house this Sunday. It will be nice to sit down for a meal with you."

I know if I decline, it will only deteriorate our relationship further. "What time?"

"You're not a goddamned visitor, and you have keys to let yourself in."

Meaning he wants me to spend the day there.

"Okay," I agree before I really try to focus on the proposal.

It's already dark out as I drive back to campus. My mind is still with the two deals, and it turned out the old file was a proposal my father wrongly invested in, which led to a huge loss.

I definitely learned a lot today, and it feels like a small part of me healed after the short talk with my father.

Piece by piece, right?

Deep in thought, I steer the car into the parking area. As I turn into the spot I always use, something crashes into my car. My body jerks, and shock rushes through me with one hell of a force.

"Fuck."

In absolute terror, I turn my head toward Jennifer.

My breaths begin to come faster as my heart pounds in my chest. I open the door and get out of the car. Feeling dazed, I somehow manage to walk to the driver's side of the other car.

Fuck, please don't let anyone be hurt.

Seeing Kingsley behind the steering wheel sends another wave of shock through me. I yank the door open and grabbing hold of her arm, I pull her out of the seat.

"Oh my gosh! I'm so sorry, Mason. I really looked before I started reversing, and the next second, bam, there you were."

I stand paralyzed, my eyes wide on Kingsley.

Slowly, the cold creeps into my bones, and I gasp for a breath of icy air.

"Mason?" she asks, her voice trembling.

The daze lifts only to be replaced by anger surging through me.

"An accident?" I hiss.

"Yes, I'm really sorry." She walks to the back of her car and looks at the damage. "Luckily, it's only a small dent."

"Small dent?" I repeat her words again.

Shaking my head, I bring my arms up and link my fingers behind my neck. I close my eyes and take a couple of breaths, but it doesn't help shit to calm me down.

Letting my arms fall to my sides, I stalk to where she's still looking at the damage, and then she mumbles, "It's just a slight bump, nothing serious."

"Slight bump?" I suck in a breath of air, then shout, "A slight fucking bump? What the fuck are you talking about?"

She swings around with wide eyes. "Don't yell at me!" She darts past me, and with stunned amazement, I watch her get back in her car. She proceeds to park the damn thing before she gets out again.

"Hunt, w-what?" I'm so fucking upset I actually begin to stammer, "What the fuck are you doing? You parked your piece of shit car?"

"Mason, I'm sorry I bumped your car," she says again. "I'll get my insurance to take care of it. Move your car. You're blocking the parking area."

Speechless, I watch her walk away from me.

I take a couple of steps after her, then remember the damn car. I quickly jog to the driver's side and park it, and getting out, I run so I can catch up with Kingsley.

I rush into her building as she swipes her keycard, opening the door to her suite. She walks inside, and before she can shut the door, I slam my hand against wood.

She lets out another annoying shriek and takes a couple of steps away from me.

I stalk inside, and slam the door shut, while anger pours off of me in waves.

"What's the problem?" she asks, giving me an incredulous look.

"It's not just a fucking bump!" I shout, unable to control the tone of my voice.

She shakes her head at me, arguing, "What do you call it? I practically nudged your car. My insurance will cover the costs."

Having zero patience left, I close my eyes, because God help me, I might do something stupid tonight.

Chapter 10

Kingsley

Mason opens his eyes, and they shimmer like smoldering coals in the dark as he stares at me.

Letting out a breath, I walk to the wall and switch on the light. Turning back to him, I ask, "What more do you want me to say? I've apologized, and I'll pay for the damage."

I can see he's struggling to stay calm, and it makes me worry whether I've triggered his memories from the past with this accident.

"It was a fucking bump that killed my sister," he grinds the words out.

Oh, my God. I did.

'There must've been a lot of blood when the branch skewered your arm to her.' I remember what West said to Mason, and it makes my stomach churn.

How could West be so cruel?

I never knew the details of the accident, only that Mason's sister died in it.

"I'm so sorry," I whisper, finally understanding why he's so upset.

My apology only seems to anger him more, because he stalks away from me, then turns back, and settles a hard glare on my face.

"She was alive. Even after we crashed into the tree, she didn't have a scratch on her." There's so much heartache on Mason's face, it makes unbelievable sadness swamp my heart.

I wish I could hug him right now.

"Then West *bumped* into us." He lets out a painfilled chuckle, and it makes tears well in my throat. "That's all it took for the branch to stab right through my arm and into her chest." Pain shudders through him as he whispers, "Just a fucking bump."

I feel so badly for him; it makes a tear slips over my cheek.

Now I understand why you've been so angry.

"I'm sorry, Mason," I say, meaning the words with all my heart.

He stares at me for a while, then asks, "Why are you crying?"

"Because I…" I don't know how to put into words that my heart is breaking for him.

He tilts his head, and I watch as the anger washes the pain from his face. "Do you pity me, Hunt?"

I do. So much.

"No," I lie because it's what he needs to hear.

He lets out a cynical burst of laughter. "You're a fucking bad liar."

"What do you want me to say?"

"Usually, you're quite good with your comebacks."

"This isn't the time for me to hit you with my sarcastic line of the day," I reply.

He's hurting so much.

"Say it," he hisses.

He begins to shake from all the emotions that must be destroying him from the inside out.

I wish I could make your pain go away.

"Say it," he shouts.

I give in, hoping if he loses his temper at me, it will help him feel better. "I can't even begin to imagine how traumatizing it must've been."

He stalks closer to me, his eyes never leaving mine.

It's okay, Mason. You can get angry at me. Just let it out.

I continue to whisper, "It's awful, and I wouldn't wish it on my worst enemy."

When he gets close, he tilts his head and asks, "Is that what I am, Hunt? Your enemy?"

I shake my head.

"Do you feel sorry for me because you think we're friends?"

I don't care what you say. Just purge yourself.

"My heart hurts for you, Mason, because no one should have to suffer through that."

"You have an answer for everything," he marvels, anger etched in hard lines over his face. "Do you ever shut up?"

Do you really want me to?

"I was scared of you, but after tonight I'm not anymore," I admit to him. "I think underneath all your assholishness, you're actually a good guy who –"

He steps right up to me and slams his hands against the wall on either side of my head.

The sudden action makes me flinch, but I lift my eyes to his, and I finish my sentence, "Who doesn't know how to deal with all the pain he mu –"

"Let me repeat myself since you're clearly deaf, Hunt. Do you ever shut the fuck up?"

Does he want me to take his mind off the pain by bickering with him?

I force my lips into a smile and answer, "Sure, I do." Bringing my hands up between us, I tick off on my fingers, as I say, "When I'm having chocolate cupcakes, chocolate donuts, oh and my favorite, cho –"

Mason grabs hold of my hands and shoves them back against the wall, and then his mouth crashes down on mine.

My heart almost jumps out of my chest as it begins to race.

Holy crap.

I didn't see this coming.

I can feel his breath on my face, and when his lips move against mine, my eyes drift closed. I wasn't lying when I said I loved his aftershave, and right now, it's all I can smell.

I never thought there would be a moment like this in my life. A moment where you need somebody to help you escape.

His tongue swipes over my bottom lip, and I open my mouth to him.

I'm not his enemy.

I'm not his friend.

But I can be a safe haven he can escape to.

Mason

I ignore all reason, and I have no excuses.

None of this makes sense, but I can't stop myself from kissing her.

She has challenged me every step of the way. She's never backed down from a fight, no matter how I tried to intimidate her. I realized all of this tonight while she was telling me how sorry she felt for me. I hated hearing those words from her. I wanted my Kingsley back, the one who never missed a beat when it came to telling me to go to hell.

Us arguing has become like a drug to me, helping me cope, helping me to forget for a moment.

And I need it so badly right now, to just escape from the past.

When Kingsley parts her lips for me, and I thrust my tongue into her mouth, my thoughts grow quiet. When she kisses me back, and her urgency begins to grow, meeting my tongue thrust for thrust, I find an outlet for all the anger, the grief, and the guilt.

She tries to pull her hands free from my hold, but instead of letting go of them, I move my hands up from her wrists and link my fingers with hers.

As the kiss turns more heated, and Kingsley nips at my bottom lip, I grin against her mouth.

Pulling slightly back, my eyes lock on hers. "Didn't take you for a biter." Her breaths come as fast as mine, her blue eyes shining like the hottest part of a flame, and it has me whispering, "Incinerate me."

She pushes against me with all her strength, and when I let her hands go, she brings them to my face and pulls me back down. Her mouth latches fiercely onto mine, and the need to take as much as I can from her grows into an uncontrollable craving.

I bring my hands to her hips and taking hold of her sweater, I begin to lift it up. Kingsley reacts by unbuttoning the top two buttons of my dress shirt before we break the kiss, and she raises her arms, so I can pull her sweater over her head.

My eyes instantly find hers and seeing them blaze with the same need, makes me move faster. I reach for her jeans and unbutton them. When the sound of the zipper going down makes her lips part, my tongue darts out, and I lick at her bottom lip before I suck it into my mouth.

As we rip each other's clothes off, our kisses turn hungry, and our breaths mingle between sucking and biting. The moment I have her naked, I grab her thighs and lift her up.

She wraps her legs around my waist, and bringing her hands to my jaw, she drags her nails over the stubble.

"Who knew you've been hiding a fucking sexy body under the layers of clothes," I breathlessly say.

I push her against the wall, and our bodies press together. Feeling her hot as fuck curves against me, has me running my hands over her sides and hips, greedy to memorize every inch.

"Fuck me, Mason," she orders, her eyes daring me to disobey.

The corner of my mouth lifts because this woman... this woman is one of a kind. She has more guts than most of the guys I know.

"This is the only time I'll ever listen to you." My voice is low and gravely, and when a smile curves around her mouth, I push my left hand between her legs and brush a finger over her opening.

Fuck, she's wet.

Tapping her against her thigh, I grumble, "Legs down."

She lets them slide, and as I kneel down, I take in the fucking amazing view of her breasts, her nipples hard.

"Open your legs," I order as I exhale a hot breath over her trimmed dark curls.

A grin slips over my face as she does what I say. I dive in and immediately begin to lap and suck at her clit.

"Holy crap," the words explode from her as her hands first fumble in my hair before she grabs fistfuls. "Ma-sss-on." Her breath catches as I drive a finger into her while scraping my teeth over her clit.

Her hands tighten in my hair, and I suck hard while I massage her inner walls.

"F-f-f-uck," she keeps gasping as if she can't remember how to breathe, and then there's silence as her body begins to shudder.

Raising to my feet, my eyes drink in the sight of her parted lips, her hooded eyes, and her flushed cheeks as she comes on my finger while I massage her clit with my palm.

When she sucks in a breath of air as if I kept her underwater for a minute, I pull my finger out of her and bring it to my mouth. Coating my lips with her arousal, I smirk when her eyes follow the movement.

I don't have to tell her what to do because her eyes come up to mine as her tongue darts out, swiping first over my top lip before she sucks my bottom lip into her mouth.

Fuck. This mouth of hers…

I pull back, and my voice sounds as if it's been put through a shredder as I ask, "Condom or pill?"

"Pill," she whispers. "Clean?"

"Tested. You?"

"Just fuck me already. My virginity is about to grow back," she sasses me.

I let out a chuckle as I take hold of her legs, lifting her up again. When her legs wrap around me, I grab hold of her ass with my left hand while using my right to position my cock at her entrance.

Our eyes lock, and I growl, "Hold on tight."

Kingsley wraps her arms around my neck, and as I enter her with one hard push, her grip on me tightens as her breath explodes from her.

Feeling her warmth around me makes a shudder ripple through my body.

Chapter 11

Kingsley

His eyes… they're filled with nothing but burning desire.

Mason Chargill.

Badass.

The CRC heir everyone fears.

And right now, he's inside of me. His eyes are on me. He's breathless because of me.

Pressing my mouth to his, one last thought drifts through me as he pulls out – he tastes like me. He thrusts back into me, hard and fast.

There's nothing gentle about this man.

He's a fighter, a hater, a fucker.

Needing air, I break the kiss. I only suck in a couple of breaths of air before Mason grabs a fistful of my hair, and yanking me forward, our mouths crash together. His teeth nip at my lips, and his tongue fights with mine while his thrusts grow harder and deeper.

Damn, this man. His kisses are as intense as his fights.

When a moan drifts from me, it makes him push harder, his thick erection stretching and massaging nerves within me, I didn't even know existed.

With his rough kisses and the way he moves in and out of me, it feels like he's trying to devour me.

And it feels soooo good.

It's not love.

It's not even hate.

It's taking and giving what we need most at this moment.

Another human's touch.

A mutual understanding that it's okay to take without making promises.

"Fuck," the word rushes into my mouth as his grip on me hardens, and he drives into me with every bit of his strength, making his muscles contract while he practically sets me alight from all the pleasure.

I let out a moan as another orgasm begins to build, and when it sweeps through me, it's so damn intense, it rips a cry from me.

Mason's body begins to tremble, and I watch as the muscles in his neck strain and his shoulders tense under my hands.

"Fuck, Hunt," he groans, pushing so deep inside me, that it makes ripples of residual pleasure trickle through me.

He empties himself with short thrusts until he ends with a final hard push, shifting my body up the wall. I drink in every inch of his face, from his smoldering eyes to his clenched jaw, while listening to the rapid breaths bursting from him.

As we come down from the high, his eyes meet mine one last time. I see the thoughts returning and how he struggles to find the right thing to say.

Feeling the need to save him, I pull my hands back from his shoulders. "As hot as that was, I need to get to the bathroom."

The corner of his mouth pulls up, and for a moment, his eyes soften.

Thank you, Hunt.

The words are written all over his face, a tender look making me drop my legs and forcing him to slip out of me.

When I walk away from him, I say, "I have a sexy ass. You should stare at it while you can."

I hear his chuckle as I disappear into my bedroom, and then I'm freaking speed walking while trying to clench my legs together.

Yeah, the not so sexy part after sex. Fun.

I catch sight of myself in the bathroom mirror and let out a snort of laughter.

Smooth, Kingsley. Real smooth. You look like a damn penguin.

Mason

I get dressed while I wait for Kingsley to finish in the bathroom. When I'm done, I gather her clothes from the floor and hearing the bathroom door open, I walk toward her bedroom.

My mind is still racing to catch up with what just happened.

Walking into the room, I see Kingsley's put on a bathrobe, so I set her clothes down on the bed.

I'm not used to feeling out of my depth, but this is a new experience for me, and I'm not quite sure how to handle it.

I've never angry fucked anyone before, and even though worry begins to stir in the back of my mind, I'll be the first to admit it was hot.

But she's Layla's best friend. She's a part of our group.

"I'll let you out," Kingsley saves me from having to be the first to speak.

We walk to the front door, but before she can open it, I do another thing I've never done before. Taking hold of the back of her neck, I pull her to my chest. I'm not the hugging kind, so instead, I press a kiss to the top of her head.

Fuck. This is going to be all kinds of awkward.

Yeah, you can say that again. You went balls deep into this mistake.

Was it really a mistake, though?

Kingsley pulls back and grins at me. "Don't take this the wrong way, but it's time for you to leave. A girl needs her beauty sleep."

Thanks for understanding.

I was wrong about you. You're actually badass.

You blew my mind.

I can't bring myself to say any of those lines. I move my hand to her face and cupping her cheek, I brush my thumb over her lips.

This mouth of yours…

She opens the door, and I pull my arm back, then walk out of her room. Not looking back, I leave her building and head straight for mine.

When I walk into the suite, Lake glances up from his phone, where he's lying on the couch.

"You only got back now?" he asks.

"Ah… yeah," I lie. "I had two proposals to look at." I move toward my room. "I'm going to sleep. G'night."

"See you tomorrow," he says, turning his attention back to his phone.

I shower and get ready for bed, my mind still humming from having sex with Kingsley.

When my light is off, and I'm staring up at the dark ceiling, the worries start to come.

How am I going to handle this tomorrow? Fuck. Things are going to be so damn awkward between us.

Was it a mistake?

The memories replay in my mind, the feel of her soft skin and sexy curves. I let out a breath as arousal begins to warm my body again. She's no longer just Kingsley, that's for sure.

Aww... fuck, how am I going to look her in the eyes without picturing her perfect tits, her absolutely fuckable ass...

Damn, that ass...

When she walked away from me, I wanted to sink my teeth into it.

I let out a groan and grabbing hold of my pillow, I yank it from under my head and shove it over my face.

"Fu-uuck! I'm so fucking fucked."

Kingsley

I'm lying in bed with a grin spread over my face.

Mason was so awkward after we had sex. The poor guy was at a loss for words.

My smile fades when I remember how he pulled me to his chest, and the kiss to the top of my head. It was so sweet, and something I never expected from Mason. And when he brushed his thumb over my lips, a tender look flashed over his face.

The sex was crazy hot and heavy, and Mason is by far the most generous lover I've ever had. Not that I've had a truckload full, but let's face it, Mason did make me orgasm twice. He didn't just take what he needed, only to leave me wanting. He gave and gave until my body was sated.

The grin quickly returns when an image of his naked body flashes through my mind. Ye-aaah, the man has been blessed in many ways. Abs for days. Shoulders... holy hell his shoulders.

I let out a moan when I remember the feel of his cock, thrusting inside of me. It might as well be a freaking magic wand because he sure created all kinds of magic with it.

"Breathe, Kingsley. You're about to overheat."

I turn onto my side, hugging my pillow to me.

Before tonight, I was still apprehensive around Mason, but after the fight and sex, I now know his bark might sound vicious, but his bite is the most erotic thing I've ever felt.

Chapter 12

Kingsley

I've made the call to my insurance company, and after writing all the details down on a sticky note, I head over to Mason's suite so I can give it to him.

Sure, I can text him the information, but there's no fun in doing that.

I knock on the door, and when Lake opens, I smile at him. "Morning. I just have something to give Mason."

"Sure." He lets me in, giving me a curious look, then he yells, "Mace!"

"What?" Mason shouts back, and seconds later, he comes walking out of his room, only wearing a pair of sweatpants. His eyes land on me, and he stops dead in his tracks, making it physically impossible for me to not grin.

I clear my throat as I walk to him, and with a straight face, I hold out the sticky note for him to take. "I called my insurance. Here are the details."

"Insurance?" Lake asks, his eyes darting between Mason and me.

Mason takes the note and stares at it for quite some time, then he mumbles, "You could've texted me."

I bite my bottom lip, so I don't tell him it wouldn't have been any fun. Unlike the absolute delight I'm having at seeing his discomfort.

"Guys," Lake says, "Insurance?"

"Oh, we had an accident," I say.

Mason tilts his head, his eyes narrowing as he glares at me.

I quickly add, "It was my fault."

"But you're both okay?" Lake asks, his eyes sharpening as he looks at us.

"Yeah, Mason was a bit upset. He yelled. I apologized." I shrug.

Mason lets out a breath he was holding, a look of relief crossing his features.

Then I add, "Then he apologized. He even got down on his knees."

Mason coughs, and under his breath, he hisses, "Shut up, Hunt."

Working hard to keep a straight face, I finish by saying, "It was the best apology ever, so all's forgiven." I walk to the door, so I can let myself out. "See you guys later."

My eyes water as I rush to the elevator, and the second I step inside, I have to grab hold of the wall to keep myself from sinking to the floor as I crack up.

That was the best conversation I've had in a long time.

Oh, God, the poor man. I'm enjoying this way too much.

Mason

"Down on your knees?" Lake asks, wagging his fucking eyebrows at me.

It feels like I just watched a trainwreck happen. Her mouth just kept going.

"Ignore her," I mutter. "She must still be in shock."

Lake lets out a bark of laughter. "From what? Seeing the size of your –"

I lunge at the fucker and wrapping an arm around his neck in a chokehold, I warn, "Don't even finish that sentence."

Lake taps at my arm. "Can't... laugh... breathe."

Letting go of him, he goes down and rolls onto his back as he cracks up.

"You... You're... Ffffffffffff."

I shake my head at him, watching him practically cry at my expense.

"Fffff..." he gasps for air and finally squeezes the words out, "Fuck frenemies."

Shaking my head, I begin to laugh. How can I not when Lake's about to piss himself, and then he says that.

Fuck frenemies.

If it weren't for the awkwardness between us, I'd definitely like to get Kingsley naked again.

The door opens, and Falcon comes into the suite, with Layla right behind him. They both stop and stare at Lake.

"What's he laughing about?" Falcon asks.

Lake points a shaking finger at me, and thank God the dude is struggling to breathe because he can't get a fucking word out.

"He saw a funny video on YouTube," I say, and crouching down next to Lake, I grab his arm and pull him to his feet. Keeping hold of Lake, I drag him toward my room.

"You're lying," Falcon replies, a smile curving around his mouth.

I push Lake into my room and say, "I'll tell you later." Shutting the door behind us, I turn to Lake. "Fucker."

Lake manages to calm down enough to say, "We need to talk." His eyes are still a watery mess, and every couple of seconds, laughter bubbles over his lips. "How did it happen?"

"What do you mean, how did it happen?" I grumble and walking over to my bed, I sit down and lean back against the headboard.

Lake comes to sit next to me. "Well, normally when a man and a wo –"

I grab a pillow and smack him hard, then I snap, "It just fucking happened."

Lake chuckles but then gathers himself. "Okay, let's be serious now."

"Yeah, sure, like that will ever fucking happen," I joke.

"No, for real, let's be serious. So, you and Kingsley had… ah… the two of you…?"

"Yes, Lake. I fucked Hunt," I admit.

My door flies open, and Falcon darts in, whispering, "You had sex with Kingsley?" He peeks out into the living room, probably checking to see where Layla is, then he looks back to me. "You are lucky Layla's using the restroom. Keep it down. We'll be out of here in five minutes." He points a finger at me. "We're so talking about this later."

He rushes back out, a smile spreading over his face. "You ready?" he asks Layla while he pulls the door shut behind him.

I stare at the closed door, and mumble, "Well, that just happened."

Lake begins to wheeze next to me. "You've written me into your will, right?"

Letting out a heavy breath, I turn my head to Lake. "Yes, Lake. If Falcon kills me tonight, you inherit everything."

Lake pats me on the shoulder and giving me a fake-ass solemn look, he says, "I'll miss you, buddy."

"Fuck off."

I've been looking all over campus for Kingsley.

She and I need to have a talk about the fucking bomb she dropped before hightailing her ass out of the suite.

I'm walking back toward her dorm, when I see her coming from the parking area, swinging a huge bag.

She looks so carefree.

She's been running circles in my mind all day, turning me fucking inside out.

I've never really looked at her. She was always just Kingsley. When I reach the entrance first, I stare at her.

I take in the sneakers on her feet, the jeans which have a huge-ass hole above her knee, and the sweater that's easily two sizes too big for her.

She has earbuds in her ears, listening to something that's making her smile. Her hair hangs loosely down her shoulders, and there's no makeup on her face.

Yeah, she's pretty in her own way, but she's still not my type.

So why did I fuck her?

Kingsley looks up, and when her eyes land on me, the smile on her face turns into a mischievous grin. She stops in front of me, and her eyes meet mine.

"Why are you smiling?" she asks, then she begins to nod. "Ahh… you planned your revenge, didn't you?" She lets out a sigh. "If you're thinking of throwing me in the pool again, just remember I can't swim for shit."

That's why.

She's different.

She's a challenge.

And her sass, damn, her sass is everything.

"Mason?" she asks, and a worried frown settles on her forehead. She steps closer to me and places her hand on my arm. "Are you okay? I'm seriously not used to you smiling."

Shaking out of my thoughts, I take a deep breath, then say, "We need to talk."

"Oh-kaaay," she points to where her suite is. "You want to come in?"

I gesture for her to go ahead.

When we walk into her suite, she goes to place the bag on the coffee table, while I shut the door.

I take a couple of steps deeper into the room. "I've been looking for you."

She digs through the bag and pulls out a lollipop. "I went to the store. I needed to restock my candy stash. I was supposed to go last night, but yeah, you know what happened."

Unwrapping the candy, she pops it in her mouth. "Want one," she mumbles around it.

"You seriously don't care what people think about you, do you?"

She shrugs and sitting down on the couch, she points to the other couch. Taking the candy from her mouth, she says, "Sit."

Yeah, let's get this over and done with. I walk to the couch and sitting down, I rest my forearms on my knees and lock eyes with her.

"Are you going to tell the entire Academy we slept together?"

Leaning forward, she grabs the wrapper and folds it around the candy, then she sets it down on the coffee table. She mirrors my position, placing her forearms on her knees, and then she gives me a smile I haven't seen before.

Is it affection?

Fuck no, I'm certain she hates my guts.

"Mason, I totally get you feel awkward, and I'm not exactly the kind of girl you're normally seen with. I was just messing with you because I knew you'd be embarrassed, and I was trying to make things easier for you."

Is she serious or joking right now?

130

Come to think of it, I don't think I've ever seen her serious.

"Are you fucking with me right now?" I ask.

"No," her lips begin to pull into a smile, "that was last night." She takes a deep breath, then continues, "I'm serious now. My best friend loves your best friend, and we can't screw with that."

I nod because I agree.

"So, I have a proposal."

"What?" I ask.

"If it bothers you that much, just pretend it never happened."

That really bothers me. "No."

Surprise flashes over her face. "No?"

"Kingsley, I'm an asshole. Everyone knows that, but I knew what I was doing when I initiated the kiss." I take a breath before I continue, "I don't want people knowing anything about my personal life."

She looks down at her hands for a while before she says, "Then you don't have anything to worry about. But honestly, if I would tell someone, it would be Layla. The same way you would share your secrets with Falcon and Lake."

"Well, Lake already knows," I mumble.

"Yeah?" she grins at me. "He's quite fast at picking up on subtle hints."

"Hunt, that wasn't a hint. The writing was on the fucking wall by the time you left."

She snorts, which is quickly followed by laughter.

"You want to know what he called us?" I ask, knowing she will get a kick out it.

She nods, trying to compose herself. "Tell me."

"Fuck frenemies."

Laughter explodes from her, and she slides off the couch.

I only realize I'm smiling when it freezes on my face as I realize why – Kingsley and Lake could've been twins.

She glances at me, and her laughter quickly dries up. "What's wrong?"

"Nothing's wrong," I say. "You just reminded me of Lake."

She chuckles, then mumbles under her breath, "Maybe one day I can remind you of me." She gets up, and when she smiles again, I almost wonder whether I just heard her murmur the words. "Well, we talked. Everything is fine. I need to study, so if you don't mind..." she gestures to the door.

132

"Sure." I walk to the door with the niggling feeling that I'm forgetting something. Shrugging it off, I open the door and let myself out.

Chapter 13

Kingsley

Walking to my class, I'm deep in thought about the conversation I had with Mason.

He doesn't regret sleeping with me, he just doesn't want anyone to know.

I'm not going to take that the wrong way. Mason can't have his personal life splattered all over for everyone to see. He at least had the decency to come talk to me.

"Kingsley," I hear Serena calling and glancing over my shoulder I see her a couple of steps behind me.

Crap.

She catches up to me, and grabbing hold of my shoulder, she turns me around and asks, "Are you avoiding me now that you're a part of the elite group?"

"No, I'm avoiding you because you've been downright mean to my best friend," I answer her honestly.

"Oh, my God. And here I thought we were all adults," she sneers, "Seems like some of us still have to grow up."

I shrug. "It is what it is, but I'm glad you realized it's time for you to grow up. You'd be doing us all a huge favor." I smile at her and give her a wave.

I turn back around to head to my class, only to come face to face with Mason and Falcon.

I take a step to the left so I can pass by them, but Mason's hand darts out, and he wraps it around the side of my neck. When he pulls me toward him, I remember how he hugged me the night before.

I'm so damn confused as I turn sideways, my eyes darting up to his face.

Keeping his hand on the side of my neck, his eyes are hard on Serena. "Are you fucking with my friends again?"

My lips part and my eyes widen as I stare at his face.

Did he just call me a friend?

"What? I can't talk to Kingsley now?" Serena crosses her arms over her chest, her eyes narrowing on Mason.

Mason surprises me again when he answers, "I'd prefer if you didn't." He pulls me closer, moving his arm around my shoulders. "You see, I have an image to uphold, and you talking to my friends..." he draws his bottom lip

135

between his teeth, then let it go before he continues, "would only taint my image."

Holy hotness.

Please bite your bottom lip again.

Serena's face sets into a dark look. "Mason, you're not the only one with a powerful father. Keep pushing me and see what happens."

A smile spreads over Mason's face, and letting go of me, he takes two steps forward. "And that's the difference between you and me." He takes hold of one of her ginger curls, giving it a look of disdain before flicking it away. "You start a war you can't handle, then you run to your daddy so he can clean up the mess." He leans closer to her. "When I start a war, I always finish it."

He glances at me from over his shoulder, "You're going to be late for class."

"Yeah, I should go." I swing back around and rush down the hallway.

Ugh. My life is becoming a freaking drama.

After my last class, I go look for Layla because I'm in serious need of some girl time.

When Layla opens her door, I make a praying gesture with my hands. "Please tell me you haven't made any plans for tonight."

"Nothing yet. I was just going to hang out. Why? Do you want to do something?" she asks, much to my relief.

With an excited face, I walk inside and ask, "Can we go somewhere off-campus. I need some girl time with my bestie."

"Sure, but where would we go?" She pulls her phone out to start searching for places.

"We can go to my family home. My dad is hardly home, and if he is, the place is so huge we won't even know he's there."

"And your mom?" she asks.

"My mom passed while giving birth to me. It's just my dad and me, so no worries."

A compassionate look softens her features. "I'm sorry, my friend."

I wave a hand. "Even though I would've liked a chance to have known her, I've dealt with it a long time ago. And my dad made sure I didn't feel like I was missing out on anything while growing up."

"I'm glad to hear that." She smiles again, then asks, Okay, when do you want to leave?"

"How soon can you be finished with packing and kissing Falcon goodbye?"

My eagerness makes laughter bubble over her lips. "Let's quickly shoot up to his suite so I can kiss him goodbye. Then we can stuff a couple of things in a bag and hit the road."

"Awesome! You're a lifesaver." I follow her out of the suite, and when we step into the elevator, I grab her arm and I do a little excited jump while letting out a squeal, "This is going to be so much fun."

"Can we get McDonald's for dinner?" she asks. "I've had a craving all week."

"We can get some on the way. Totally my treat."

"And a milkshake," she adds.

"Done," I say as we stop in front of the door.

Layla knocks, and we both grin at Lake when he opens the door.

"My girls," he smiles at us. "You look like you've just planned a murder and got away with it."

"Nope, we planned a girls night out," Layla answers. "Is Falcon here?"

Lake tips his head toward Falcon's bedroom. "Last time I checked, he was showering."

"In that case, I'll wait in the living room," I tease Layla, winking at her.

She chuckles as she walks to his bedroom, and after knocking, she lets herself in.

"So, what's your plan for ladies' night?" Lake asks when we sit down.

"Junk food, binge-watching something funny, aaaannnddd probably some more junk food."

Lake smiles. "Do I have to wear a dress so I can join you?"

"If you do facials with us, and I get to paint your nails hot pink, then it's a deal."

"Facials, yes. Hot pink, solid no."

I pout playfully, "No fun."

His eyes dart to something behind me, but before I can look, Mason jumps over the back of the couch and ends up sitting right beside me.

"Where do you put all the junk you eat?" he asks, resting an arm behind me on the couch.

I lean forward and glance back at him. "It all goes into energy to create comebacks for whenever we go at each other."

I feel him tug at my hair, and can't help but frown.

What's going on?

Yes, we had sex, but it was a heat of the moment thing.

I thought we'd just go back to the way things were. But after the encounter with Serena, and now him sitting next to me and tugging at my hair?

Damn… way to screw with a girl's mind, Dude.

He brings his other hand to my face, and I pull back, which makes the corner of his mouth curl up. He brushes a finger over my forehead. "Stop frowning, Hunt."

"Then stop being so weird," I say. "It's… it's… weird."

A smile stretches over his face, and it only makes me look at him like he lost his mind. "Did you smoke some weed? Drank a little too much?"

He leans into me and feeling his breath on my ear, he whispers, "Payback for this morning." He pulls a little back, and our eyes lock. "Watching you squirm is way more fun than getting you all riled up."

"Ahh… is that so?" I tilt my head and close the distance between us again. When I'm so damn close to his mouth that my lips begin to tingle, I repeat his words from this morning in a seductive whisper, "Careful, Mason. When I start a war, I always finish it."

His lips pull in to a sexy grin, which has the power to melt a thousand panties.

Okay, maybe I won't win the war, but damn, as long as he grins like that while wiping the floor with me, it will be worth it.

"Is that a dare I hear, Hunt?" His voice is so low and rough, it sounds the same as when he was deep inside of me.

"Uhm… guys." Lake gets up, pulling us out of the moment. I quickly pull away from Mason. "You don't want to move this to the bedroom?" Lake asks, and when we look at him, he smiles, "Daddy doesn't need to see this."

"Falcon and Layla also don't need to see it," Falcon teases behind me.

I shoot up from the chair, and when I see the huge smile on Falcon's face and Layla's eyes wide with surprise, I say, "Let's go, Layla." I hold my hand out to her. "Before I do something stupid."

She presses a kiss to Falcon's mouth, and whispers, "I'll text you when we get there."

Taking my hand, she wags her eyebrows at me, "Something stupid like… ?"

"There's a strong possibility I might bite someone," I say as I glance at Mason, who still has the grin plastered all over his face, which makes me add, "And there will be blood."

141

"Kinky, Hunt," Mason chuckles. "Careful, I might hold you to that."

Frazzled because he's teasing me and not biting my head off, I drag Layla to the door.

"We better go before we get whatever bug Mason has," I mumble as I drag her out and down the passage.

Layla laughs her ass off all the way down to the bottom floor.

"You have a lot to tell me," she says as we step out of the elevator. "What happened between you and Mason?"

"Angry sex," I mumble.

Layla's eyes grow huge with surprise, and opening her door to the suite, she says, "What? And you're only telling me now?"

"It only happened two days ago," I explain.

"I have to admit, my friend, I never thought I'd see you and Mason end up together," she says while shoving a couple of things into a bag, "but, damn, it sure is fun watching you and Mason fall for each other."

"We're not falling for each other," the words burst from me, which makes Layla wag her eyebrows at me.

"It's only a matter of time before it strikes you like a lightning bolt, and you realize you're head over heels for the guy."

"If that lighting bolt hits me, it will only end up frying my ass. Never in a ka-zillion years will Mason fall for me."

Sobering up, Layla asks, "What makes you say that?"

"I'm not his type."

Layla grabs the bag, and we lock her suite before heading to mine. She throws her arm around my shoulder and says, "Like I said, it's going to be one hell of an awesome show watching the two of you fall for each other."

Chapter 14

Mason

The second the girls are gone, Falcon asks, "Is this thing between you and Kingsley serious?"

"Nah, I'm just fucking with her."

"Literally," Lake mumbles under his breath.

Falcon stares at me, and a smile begins to form on his face.

Knowing exactly what he's thinking, I quickly defend, "It's nothing like that."

"You're at stage three. Don't worry, it passes quickly," Lake says as he lies down on the couch.

"Stage three? Do I even want to hear this?"

"Stage one, fighting. Stage two, you either kiss or in your case, become fuck frenemies. Stage three, denial. Stage four, you realize you like the girl but then have no idea what to do. Stage five, you take the plunge, and it's game over for your bachelor status."

I look to Falcon and grinning the fucker nods. "I'm afraid he's right."

I let out a chuckle and shake my head. "That will never happen. When it comes to Hunt, there are only two stages, fighting or fucking, but definitely no denial and taking a plunge."

Lake sighs loudly. "Like I said. Denial."

"Don't worry," Falcon says, and he leans over so he can pat me on the shoulder. "You'll survive."

"Yeah?" I ask as I grab his arm and yank him to me. I wrestle him to the ground, growling, "Can't promise you'll survive."

It's been a quiet weekend with the girls gone.

Falcon's been working on the business plans, and Lake's been talking with Lee-ann. She's arriving next month, and I really hope it turns out well for Lake.

I park my car in the driveway and getting out, my eyes sweep over my family home.

There's the familiar grip of grief around my heart, but it's not as tight as before.

I let myself into the house and go up the stairs to Jen's room. I stop outside the bedroom and take a deep breath before I open the door.

The first thing I notice is that the smell has changed. Jen's scent no longer hangs in the air.

I walk over to her dresser and pick up the perfume she used. Bringing the bottle to my nose, I close my eyes.

'What are you doing in my room?' Jen asks, catching me red-handed while I take a photo of the perfume she likes, so I can get it for her birthday.

Grabbing the first thing in sight, I hold it up. 'I wanted to borrow this.'

'A scrunchie? For what?'

Shit. I stare at the scrunchie, then do the only thing I can think of. I gather my hair at the top and struggle to tie it, but finally succeed... sort of.

'Really?' she grins while crossing her arms.

'Yeah, I want to see if a man bun would work for me.'

'I dare you to go to school like that tomorrow.'

I yank the thing out and drop it on her dresser. 'No, way. Falcon and Lake will never let me live it down.'

Her laughter follows me as I rush out of her room.

Opening my eyes, I look at all the photos she stuck to the side of her mirror. Seeing one of us, pulling faces at the camera, I reach for it.

"You were the best sister," I whisper.

I go to sit down on her bed and keep staring at her face.

"Would you hate me if I moved on?"

Hearing movement, my head snaps up. My mother's leaning against the door jamb. There's a soft smile around her mouth, and I can't even remember when last I saw it.

She glances around the room, then says, "I wanted to put her things in storage but waited for you to come to say goodbye."

"Storage?" I ask, not liking the sound of that.

"Yes." Mom walks closer and sits down next to me. She leans in and looks at the photo. "This room feels like a tomb. I don't want to remember Jennifer this way – as if time froze."

Mom brings her eyes to my face, and she smiles warmly. Reaching for my hair, she brushes her fingers through it, and it makes emotion well in my chest.

Tears begin to fill her eyes, and with a trembling voice, she whispers, "It's time I focus on my son. He's still here with me."

I can't keep the emotion from engulfing me, and it makes a tear roll over my cheek.

Mom lets out a shaky breath, and she wipes my tear away with the gentle touch I've missed for so long.

"I'm sorry I was such a shitty mother when you needed me most."

"You had your own pain," I whisper.

She shakes her head. "You're my child, and you should've come first."

Dropping her hand to mine, she pulls the photo from my fingers and sets it aside, before holding my hand tightly.

"Jennifer will always be my daughter, my perfect angel. Moving on doesn't mean we're forgetting her. She'll always be a part of who we are because she helped shape us."

Mom brings her other hand to my chest and pats over my heart. "Carry her here and live the life she wanted for you." Moving her hand to my hair, she again brushes her fingers through the strands. "Don't carry her here where you're trapped in the past."

Another tear sneaks down my cheek and closing my eyes, I let the peace which only my mother's touch can give me, fill my heart.

When my shoulders shudder under the heavyweight of the emotions, Mom wraps her arms around me, and rubbing her hand over my back, she whispers, "It's okay, Mace. I just got lost, but I'm here now. Mom's here."

———————————

Sitting at the table out on the patio, I watch my father grill steaks.

"Since when do you grill?" I ask, still shocked by seeing my father make food. "Is it going to be edible?"

Dad turns around and points at me with the tongs. "It's a new hobby."

Mom lets out a chuckle. "He has grilled just about everything." She lets out a snort of laughter, and I can only stare at her in awe. "He tried to grill marshmallows." She cracks up, unable to tell me the rest of the story.

Dad lets out a sigh. "What your mother is trying to tell you is that I tried to roast marshmallows, but it melted, and the entire grill was a mess."

"A mess?" Mom squeezes out. "You had to get a new grill!"

I sit back and smile as I watch my parents. There's a sweet ache in my chest, seeing them the way they were before Jen's passing.

Piece by piece.

Kingsley

We've just gotten back to campus, and I feel a million times better. Spending time with Layla has grounded me.

We stop outside my dorm, and I pull Layla into a hug. "Thanks, my bestie. I had a great time," I whisper, tightening my hold on her for a second before I pull back.

"We have to do this again, and soon. I want to finish watching *Grace & Frankie*." She chuckles, "I can just see the two of us being like them when we're old."

"Yeah," I agree. "I'd probably be the one smoking weed."

Layla laughs, then gives my arm a squeeze. "Let me go give my man some tender love and care. I'll see you in class tomorrow."

"Enjoy the TLC." I wag my eyebrows at her and smiling, I walk into the building.

My smile dies a quick death when I see Serena walking towards me.

Her lips form a well-rehearsed smile. "I didn't know you went away for the weekend."

"Yeah."

I begin to walk toward my suite when Serena grabs hold of my arm. "Please take a walk with me. If we're going to stop being friends, I'd like to hear the reason for it."

If she wants to have this conversation, then so be it, but she's not going to like what I have to say. Not wanting her in my suite, I nod. "Let me just throw my bag in my room."

She waits as I quickly open the door and toss the bag inside. When I get back to her, I gesture for her to lead the way.

Leaving the dorm, we walk toward the restaurant.

"So, you're really going to end our friendship because I don't get along with Falcon's assistant?"

Frowning, I correct her, "Her name is Layla. You know the girl Falcon's in a serious relationship with? My best friend?"

"Whatever," she snubs my words away, then taking hold of my arm, she pulls me toward the indoor pool. "I can see this is not going to be a civil conversation, so let's go where the other students won't hear us arguing. I don't want them seeing how much it will break my heart to lose you."

Huh?

"Did you drink?" I ask her as we walk into the room. Not liking the darkness, I turn on the light while Serena goes to stand by the pool and stares at the water. I stop a couple of steps behind her and cross my arms over my chest.

"It's funny how quickly I was rejected when *she* came to Trinity," Serena murmurs.

"It's not because of Layla. You're not a nice person, Serena. People have to jump through hoops to please you."

She turns around and begins to sneer, the oh-woe-is-me act gone. "You're so great now that Mason is paying some attention to you? Do you honestly believe Mason will ever be with a girl like you?"

That was such a quick change of topic, I stare at her as I try to process it.

"We're not talking about Mason and me. We're talking about why I won't be friends with you any longer."

She ignores my words, and taking a step closer to me, she smugly says, "You know I'm more his type."

"Right. I must've forgotten the two of you were on good terms," I reply, a cynical smirk forming on my face.

"We were," she says, and for a moment she just stares at me. "Until you and that assistant came along, I had them eating out of the palm of my hand."

"Them? Did you change the subject again? Because we're definitely not talking about Falcon, Mason, and Lake right now." I take a step closer to her. "You need to accept none of the heirs to CRC will ever be interested in you."

Her mouth pulls down at the corners, and her eyes sweep over me with disdain. "As if any of them will even look at you twice. Money certainly can't buy class."

"I'm done having this conversation with you. Stay away from my friends, Serena. I might not be as wealthy as you, but I give a mean bitch-slap."

Before I can turn to leave, she grabs my arm and yanks me toward her. It catches me off guard, and as I stumble, she steps to the side.

Shit, she wouldn't.

Shock vibrates through me when she shoves me into the pool.

I see the smirk on her face.

The gleam in her eyes.

And then the water closes around me before I can take a breath.

Chapter 15

Mason

I just got back to campus and see Layla coming out of the dorm.

"You're back," I say as I catch up to her. "Are you heading to the restaurant?"

"Yeah, we got back five minutes ago. I just called Falcon, and he's busy feeding Lake. Have you eaten?" she asks as we begin to walk.

"My father tried to grill steaks." I shudder when I think of the overdone steak. "He wasn't very successful, so I'm starving."

"Besides starving, did you have a nice day with your parents?" Layla asks.

I'm surprised how easy it is to admit to her. "Yeah, I did."

She pats me on the arm. "I'm really glad to hear that, Mason."

I look at Layla, and I think it's the first time I actually smile at her. "Have I told you I think you're a great person?"

"You have now," she grins, then she teases, "But if you want to tell me some more, I won't stop you."

"I'm glad Falcon has you."

"Thanks, Mason. It means a lot coming from you."

She sees something behind me and ducks to her left, using my body to hide behind. "Don't move. It's Serena," she whispers. "Hopefully, she won't see us."

A full-blown smile stretches over my face as I watch Layla peek around my right side.

Then she straightens up. "The coast is clear."

I chuckle. "Come on, let's go see what the guys are up to."

"Well, Lake's probably up to his neck in pizza."

"True, very true."

I glance around us as we walk, and through the windows of the indoor pool, movement in the water catches my eye.

"Isn't that Lake's assistant?" I ask Layla. "The guy in the pool. What's his name again?"

"To be honest, I don't know. I haven't seen him since the ball, and he wasn't introduced to me."

"It was a soiree," I correct her.

"That was a ball," she argues wryly, then she frowns as she glances past me to the pool house. "It looks like he needs help."

Layla begins to walk toward the pool, and I follow right behind her.

The guy must see us, because he starts to yell, "Help! I need help!"

Instinctively I shoot forward, running until I get to closer to the pool. "Are you okay?" I ask as I get close to him.

"She drowned," the guy cries, panic all over his face. "I can't lift her out."

Fuck.

Luckily, the guy has her head resting on his shoulder, but all I can see is wet black hair. Crouching by the edge of the pool, I reach down and hooking my hands under her arms, I pull her up.

"What happened?" Layla asks.

"Call security. Tell them to hurry over," I say to Layla before I move back so I can get the girl totally out of the water.

"Tell them a girl –" As I lay her down, my eyes dart to her face, and the shock hits so fucking hard, it knocks me onto my ass.

It's only a second, and then adrenaline clears my head at lightning speed. I dart forward and wipe the hair away from her face. "Hunt!"

Her lips are blue.

Fuck, no.

My head swings to Layla, who's standing frozen, her eyes huge on her friend. "Make the call, Layla!" I shout, and it snaps her out of the moment of shock.

Touching my fingers to Kingsley's pulse, dread creeps over me when I can't feel anything. I move my hands to her chest and begin with compressions.

I've had some first aid training because we like to go surfing, but fuck, that was a couple of years ago.

"Shouldn't we give her air?" Layla asks as she kneels on the other side of Kingsley.

I stop pressing on Kingsley's chest and blow two breaths into her mouth before I resume the compressions. My words are breathless from fear, as I ask, "Is security coming?"

"Yes."

My eyes go to Kingsley's face and seeing her blue lips again, make horrifying shivers race over my body.

Don't die.

Please.

Don't die.

I press harder on her chest, and as time crawls by, I keep pushing harder, unwilling to give up.

"Come on, Hunt," I whisper. "Hold on."

Layla picks up Kingsley's hand and holds it to her chest while sobs wrack her body.

I've forgotten about Lake's assistant until I hear him scream, "Over here! She's over here!"

Seconds later, Layla moves out of the way, and a security guard takes her place. "Let me take over," he instructs.

I can't bring myself to stop, and Layla has to grab hold of me and pull me away. She doesn't let go of me, keeping her arms wrapped around me as she cries against my back.

I feel paralyzed as I watch the security guard work on Kingsley.

How did this happen?

Why?

Why Kingsley?

Thoughts swamp my mind, only adding to the torture.

She's so fucking young.

She had so much life in her.

I can't stand the thought that I'll never see her smile again. I'll never hear her laughter again.

Time warps as more people rush into the room.

I stare at Kingsley's face until she becomes a blur as tears flood my eyes.

It feels like I've lost something important.

Numbly, I reach for her hand, and when I feel how cold her skin is, my heart shatters.

This girl. Oh, God.

This girl has been torn from my heart, and I didn't even know she'd filled it with her cheerfulness. Fuck, I'd give anything to have her open those blue eyes and to hear her sass me.

I'd give my life, because what is life when the sun has been ripped from the sky?

I can't remember the trip to the hospital or what happened the two days after Kingsley was admitted. I can't remember anything but Kingsley's pale face.

She looked like death.

Sitting next to her bed in the private room her father arranged for her, I hold her hand between both of mine, unable to tear my eyes away from her face.

I'm just glad Dr. Hunt allowed us to stay with Kingsley. He's been here whenever he could get away from work. I don't know how he's able to function while his daughter almost drowned, and she hasn't woken yet.

Every breath the machine forces into her.

Every beep echoing her heart.

It's torture. It's fucking killing me.

"Mason." Falcon places his hand on my shoulder. "Can I get you anything?"

I blink, and it makes my eyes burn. "No."

He walks to the other side of the bed and hugs Layla to him. I hear her start to cry again. I wasn't even aware she stopped.

"Shh... I've got you," he whispers to her.

"How?" Layla whimpers. "How did this happen? I saw her walk into her dorm. Why would she go to the pool?"

"She'll tell us what happened when she wakes up," Falcon whispers.

I feel a hand on my shoulder, and I don't have to look to know it's Lake.

"You were right." My voice sounds raw. "I was in denial."

Lake wraps his arm around me from behind.

My breathing begins to speed up, and pressing my forehead to her fingers, I whisper, "I won't survive it a second time." My body begins to shiver uncontrollably as futile hopelessness seeps into my heart.

"She's going to wake up," Lake whispers right by my ear. "Kingsley's a fighter. She will wake up."

Fuck. Please let Lake be right.

Please.

I want the chance to see the surprise on her face when I tell her the impossible happened. I fell for a feisty girl with zero style. I fell for the smile, which used to annoy me.

I fucking fell... too late.

Chapter 16

Mason

I'm not sure where the others went, but the room is quiet with only the sounds coming from the life support.

Even though the doctors said all the tests suggested there should be no permanent damage, I can't help but fear for the worst.

I lean my cheek against the back of her hand. "I need you to wake up." I swallow hard on the lump that's stuck in my throat since I pulled her out of the water. "Open your eyes." I stare at her face, looking for any hint that she can hear me.

"Kingsley," I whisper. "Please."

When her fingers lightly move in my hands, my breath is knocked from my lungs.

"Did you just move?" I dart from the chair and sit on the side of the bed. Bracing my hands on either side of her head, I lean closer. My eyes search her face for a sign that she's waking up.

Seconds become minutes, and the brief hope I felt is crushed. I want her to wake up so badly, I must've imagined it.

Then her eyes flutter, and when she finally opens them, it feels like the sun is breaking through the long dark night that's been my life for the past three days.

I reach down for her hand and holding it, I ask, "Can you hear me? Just squeeze."

Her fingers stir weakly, but it's enough to make relief chase the dread away, making me feel dizzy.

Her eyes drift closed, and I bring her fingers to my mouth, pressing a kiss against them.

Thank you.

Fuck. Thank you for not dying.

The door opens, and Falcon comes in with Layla right behind him

"Did something happen?" he asks because I'm still sitting on the bed.

A relieved smile tugs at my lips. "She opened her eyes. She indicated that she could hear me."

164

"She did!" Layla darts past Falcon and grabs Kingsley's other hand. "She woke up?" she asks me, a hopeful look on her face.

I nod, and moving back to the chair, I rest my forehead against the bed. "She woke up."

Placing Kingsley's hand back down, Layla says, "I'll go get a nurse."

I didn't even think to do that.

Minutes later, Layla returns with a nurse, who checks Kingsley's vital signs.

"We'll check with the doctor to see if the tubes can come out," the nurse mentions. When she sees my worried eyes on her, she adds, "It's a good sign that she woke up, but it's still early days. All you can do now is wait and let her heal."

I know she's right, but it doesn't make the waiting any easier.

Kingsley

For the longest time, it feels as if I swallowed so much water, it drowned my brain. Everything is blurry.

I'm aware of people coming and going, but it seems like forever passes before I can finally open my eyes.

When my gaze focuses on Dad's face, he smiles gently at me.

"Hey, Tiger," he whispers while getting up from the chair. His hold on my hand tightens, and leaning over me, he presses a kiss to my forehead. "How are you feeling?"

"B-b…" My throat hurts, and my voice sounds raspy. I begin to cough, and Dad quickly moves back. He pats my shoulder until the bout of coughing dies down, and then only am I able to whisper, "Better."

A nauseous feeling pushes up my throat, and I swallow a couple of times before I ask, "How long was I out?"

"Almost four days." My dad looks like he's aged a hundred years.

"I'm sorry."

He shakes his head and forces a smile to his face. "Nothing to be sorry for, Tiger." His eyes brush over my face, then he asks, "What happened? How did you fall in the pool?"

Before I can answer, the door opens, and Mason walks in, with Layla right behind him.

Mason freezes when he sees I'm awake, while Layla darts forward. Dad moves back to give her space as she gently hugs me.

"I was so worried," she says, her voice thick with tears. Slightly pulling away, she asks, "Do you feel okay?"

I nod and try to keep the weak smile on my face when Layla's face crumbles. She brings her hand up to cover her mouth.

"Come here," I whisper. When she hugs me again, I try to pat her side, but I'm so weak, I'm not sure she feels it. "It's okay. I'm fine."

She shakes her head and keeps hugging me for a while before she pulls back. Moving away from the bed, she gestures to Mason. "Come."

He shakes his head, staying close to the door.

"I have to go to the office quickly," Dad says. "It won't take long. I'll stop by the house to get a couple of things for you. Is there anything specific you want?"

I shake my head. "No, just you…" I have to pause to catch my breath before I can continue, "to come back quickly."

Leaning over me, he presses another kiss to my forehead. "I'll be as quick as a flash. I love you, Tiger."

"Love you, Dad."

Dad stops by the door and looking at Layla, then Mason, he says, "Thank you for watching over my girl."

Layla smiles at Dad, where Mason just nods.

I watch Dad leave, then turn my head back to Layla, as she says, "I'm going to call Falcon and Lake. They'll be happy to hear you're awake."

I nod, and when she leaves, I look at Mason, who is still standing in the same spot by the door.

Our eyes lock, and a couple of seconds pass before he moves toward me. He stops near my feet and places a hand on my shin. It looks like he's hesitating, which I'm totally not used to seeing.

Then he squares his shoulders and rushing forward, he grabs hold of my shoulders and lifts me to his chest, his arms wrapping around me.

"Oomph!" I'm surprised by his behavior and how tightly he's holding me.

Then he turns his face into my neck as he sits down on the side of the bed so he can hold me better. I lift my right hand to his back and brush it lightly over his sweater.

Quite a while later, he whispers, "You scared the fucking shit out of me."

I let out a breathless burst of laughter. "That's hard to believe."

His arms tighten around me, and then he presses a kiss to my neck. My eyebrows pop up, and my hand freezes on his back.

Was he really that scared?

Because of me?

He lays me back down, but then surprises me, even more, when he frames my face with his hands. His eyes search over me as if he doesn't quite believe that I'm okay.

"Mason, I'm fine." I let a weak smile form around my dry lips. "Stop fretting." I take a couple of breaths, then continue, "I'm not used to you fussing over anything."

The corner of his mouth lifts, and it might be because I'm still out of it, but I can swear there's warmth in his gaze.

"Can you do me a favor and tell me to go to hell?"

With an eyebrow lifting, I ask, "Dude, why?" I shake my head, which is still cupped in his hands. "Oh, wait…" I hate that I can't say a couple of words without becoming breathless, "maybe this is … some weird-ass dream." My chuckle sounds more like a wheeze before I finally finish, "There's no way … you'd be so nice to me … in real life."

"Have I been that big of an asshole?" he asks, a smile stretching over his face.

"I just drowned," I complain.

169

"Almost," he corrects me.

"I almost drowned," I say wryly. "Give me … a break."

Nausea tightens my stomach and pushes up my throat again. I swallow a couple of times before the feeling subsides a little.

"I'm not back … to full capacity yet." I try to grin. "Honestly, I don't know … how to react … to you not growling … at me."

"Okay," he agrees. There's a weird look on Mason's face as if it hurts him to see me struggling to talk.

Maybe he's just tired.

He pulls away but remains sitting next to me on the bed. Picking up my hand, he wraps his fingers around mine, then rests our hands on his thigh. "I'll ease up on the nice. Can we talk about what happened? Do you remember?"

My memories are foggy, but I remember one thing clearly, and it makes anger and hurt wash over me. "Serena."

My breathing begins to rush over my lips as I recall how she yanked me toward her before pushing me into the pool. The beeping from the machine monitoring my heart speeds up, and when a coughing fit overwhelms me, Mason pulls me slightly forward so he can pat my back.

170

"It's okay," he says. "We don't have to talk about it now."

The coughing subsides, and I take a couple of deep breaths.

Then I remember the smirk on her face and the gleam in her eyes, and it makes an awful feeling shudder through me.

"She ... pushed me." The words are nothing more than a whisper filled with disbelief. My eyes meet Mason's, and he brings his hand back to my face, brushing his fingers lightly over my cheek. Doubting my memories, I ask, "Did she really ... try to kill me?"

A look filled with hurt and anger tightens his features. "It was caught on camera. Security gave me the footage yesterday."

Oh, my God. I never thought she'd go that far.

Some of the details leading up to my near-drowning shudder through me, and it makes me feel unbelievably vulnerable. My bubble of safety pops, making me feel exposed and threatened.

Mason must see the distress on my face because he leans over me and braces his arms on either side of my head. He locks eyes with me, and says, "I've got you, Hunt.

I'll take care of Serena. I promise I'm going to make her pay."

A sob pushes up my throat, and it makes it harder to breathe.

Mason moves his left hand to my head, and he begins to brush repeatedly over my hair. "I'm here, babe."

My chest aches as I keep my eyes locked on his until tears blur my sight.

I can't say anything and quickly blink the tears away so I can see Mason's face.

She tried to kill me.

As if he can read my thoughts, he answers, "I'm going to make her pay."

I'm scared.

"I'm not leaving. I've got you."

Promise.

"You're stuck with me, Hunt."

My erratic breaths calm down, and it takes a lot of strength for me to lift my arm. Placing my hand on the back of Mason's, I move his palm to my cheek. Turning my head slightly, I breathe in his scent.

I've never been one to hold grudges or to condone violence, but she tried to take my life.

172

"I want her … to pay." My voice trembles from the disturbing emotions overwhelming me. "I want her … to pay…" I swallow hard on the nauseous lump in my throat, then finish, "for what's … she's done to me."

Mason leans closer, and his words are in total contrast to the caring warmth in his eyes. "I'm going to destroy her."

I nod and begin to feel drowsy from all the unwanted excitement.

Mason might be an asshole, but he's a powerful asshole, and right now, I need him more than anyone else. I need him to keep me safe while I can't protect myself. But mostly, I need him to take revenge for me because bitch-slapping that woman just won't cut it.

When I feel him move back, my eyes snap open, and my breathing begins to speed up again. "Don't leave."

He leans back over me and pressing his forehead to mine, he whispers, "I won't. Sleep, babe." He presses a kiss to the corner of my mouth. "I won't let anyone hurt you again. You're safe."

I drift off while feeling Mason's breath fan over my face as he keeps reassuring me I'm safe.

Chapter 17

Mason

"I thought Layla would come," Kingsley mentions once I have her settled in the car. "Not that I'm ungrateful for you coming."

"I asked Layla to do something for me," I answer as I start the engine. Pulling away from the hospital, absolute relief washes over me. I just want to get Kingsley away from this place.

When she doesn't question what I asked Layla to do, I quickly glance at her before looking at the road again. She's just gazing out the window, which prompts me to ask, "Are you okay?"

"Huh?" She turns her head to me with a questioning look.

"Are you okay?" I repeat the question.

"Oh, yeah, I'm fine."

She goes back to gazing out the window, which has me worried. Kingsley normally talks my ear off.

I get us back to the Academy as quickly as I can without breaking any traffic laws and stop in front of the dorm. Getting out, I jog around the front of the vehicle and open Kingsley's door.

She's busy pulling her bag onto her lap and stops to give me another questioning look. "What?" She glances at the driver's side then asks, "Did you forget something?"

I crouch down and place my hand on her knee, a worried frown settling on my brow. "Are you sure you're okay?"

"Dude, I said I'm fine." When she glares at me, it brings a smile to my face.

"Why aren't you getting out of the car then?" I ask.

"When you opened the door, I thought you forgot something, and you wanted me to grab it for you."

Finally realizing what has her confused, I smile even wider. "Hunt, I opened the door, so you could get out."

"Huh?" She looks at me as if I've grown two heads, and it makes me laugh, because her not knowing how to respond to me being kind to her, is funny.

I reach for her bag and standing up, I throw it over my shoulder while I hold a hand out to her.

175

She glares at me again, and placing her hand in mine, she mumbles, "Just so you know, this is weird."

When she's out of the car, I don't let go of her hand, and say, "Shut the door, please. My hands are full."

She begins to pull her hand away, which has me lacing our fingers and tightening my grip.

"Hunt, the door," I repeat.

It's easier fucking with her by being friendly than when I fought with her.

She finally slams the door closed, and I begin to walk, slowing my strides to match her shorter steps. When we walk toward the Hope Diamond's entrance, Kingsley rears back.

"I just want to get into bed. I'll greet everyone later."

"Okay," I say, but I still keep heading toward the entrance.

She tries to pull her hand free, and when she doesn't succeed, she whacks me against the arm. "Mason!"

"Hu-unt."

She darts in front of me and placing a hand against my chest, she forces me to stop. She lifts an eyebrow and gestures with a nod of her head to our linked hands as she brings them up between us.

"What's going on here?"

176

The corner of my mouth lifts into a grin. "Oh, I moved you to the Hope Diamond."

A look of surprise washes over her features. "Say what now?"

"Your suite is no longer in the Pink Star. Your stuff has been moved to the Hope Diamond. That's what Layla was helping me with."

"Whyyyy?" she asks, giving me a puzzled look.

I let go of her hand and bringing mine up, I wrap my fingers around the back of her neck. Leaning a little down, I say, "Because I made you a promise to keep you safe, Hunt. I want you in the same building as me."

With her eyes locked on mine, her lips part, and she sucks in a deep breath. "You meant it?"

I pull her closer as I begin to walk again and rest my arm around her shoulders. "I never say anything I don't mean."

We're about to pass Layla's old suite, when Kingsley says, "Let me just say hi to Layla."

"She's been moved as well."

"What? To where?" Kingsley asks as she glances up at me with wide eyes.

"The three of you are now on the floor below my suite," I answer her as I press the button for the elevator.

"Three of us?"

"You," I say, pulling her into the elevator, "Layla and Lake's assistant, Preston."

"Oh," she shrugs, which has me moving my hand back to her neck. "Well, I suppose that makes sense, having all three assistants near you."

The doors open on her floor, and we step out. "It's so no one else can fuck with the three of you."

"Oh."

We stop in front of her suite, and I open the door. When Kingsley walks in, everyone shouts, "Welcome back!"

Preston's blowing on a party whistle, while shaking his ass, and waving his arms in the air. Kingsley only manages to take a couple of steps inside when he ditches the whistle and plowing into her, he hugs her.

"I'm so glad you didn't die," he almost cries.

"Oh-kaaay?" Kingsley stands frozen with a get-the-dude-off-me look all over her face.

I walk by them and set her bag down by the couch, then say, "Preston found you. He saved your life."

"What?" Shock ripples over her face and she pulls back to look at Preston. "You saved me?"

"I just kept your head above water," he answers, looking embarrassed. He takes a step back and glances down at the floor while shoving his hands in his pockets.

"Just?" Kingsley whispers. A grateful smile makes her look so fucking beautiful, and then a tear slips over her cheek. She takes a step closer to Preston and wrapping her arms around his waist, she hugs him. "Thank you, Preston. Thank you so much."

He lets out a nervous chuckle before he hugs her again. "I'm just really glad you're better."

"Okay, that's enough. Daddy needs to see his little girl," Lake says, instantly breaking the heavy feeling in the room.

Preston lets go of Kingsley and comes to stand at my side.

Lake practically engulfs Kingsley. "I'm glad you're back." He presses a kiss to the side of her head, and letting go of her, he asks, "So what do you think of your new place?"

Kingsley glances around, then smiling, she replies, "I love it. Thanks for moving my stuff, guys."

Leaning my head closer to Preston, I whisper, "How did the test run go?"

Bringing his hand up, he holds it in front of his mouth and whispers back. "I managed to hack into their system. It took them over ten minutes to block me."

"Good, we only need four minutes." I pat his shoulder and walking to Kingsley, I say, "Glad you're home, Hunt." I glance at Falcon and Lake. "I have something to take care of. I'll catch you later."

Putting my hand on Kingsley's back, I press a kiss to the side of her head, which has her freezing. "Don't overdo it, and get some rest. I'll check on you later."

I don't give her time to respond and walk out of the suite. Taking the elevator down, I pull out my phone and dial Serena's number as I head out of the building.

The rage, which keeps building with every day I have to hold back, boils inside of me like lava in a volcano.

"Yes, Mason?" she answers.

"Where are you?"

"At the restaurant on campus. I'm having lunch. Why?"

I end the call and stalk toward the restaurant. I haven't said a word to her since Kingsley's near-drowning. Right now, Serena thinks she got away with hurting someone I care about... again.

But that's about to change. Today she starts paying, and it will all lead up to the grand finale I've arranged just for her.

Entering the restaurant, I head over to the table she's sharing with some other girls. I stop next to her and glancing over everyone, I bite out, "Leave."

The girls scatter, and quickly rush away. I pull one of the chairs closer to Serena and sitting down, I rest my left arm next to her half-eaten salad.

A smile forms around my mouth, and I stare at her. She lets out an irritated sigh while dropping her napkin on the table. "To what do I owe this honor."

I keep smiling, my eyes not leaving hers... until she looks away.

Leaning forward, I move into her personal space. Restrained anger makes my voice drop low as I growl, "I warned you."

"What did I do this time?" she sneers while giving me an annoyed look.

I sit back again and tilt my head. "You made Falcon's life a living hell by stalking him. You gave Layla a spiked pie, and it almost killed her."

The irritated look on her face deepens, and when her mouth begins to curve up, it takes all of my strength to not hit her. I dart forward and grabbing hold of the back of her neck, I yank her face close to mine. My voice is nothing more than a deadly growl. "You should've stopped there, and I would've taken it easy on you. But almost killing Kingsley... you fucked up big time by going after my woman." I let go of her so quickly she falls back against her chair, her breaths rushing over her parted lips and her eyes wide with fear.

That's right, bitch. Be afraid, because I'm going to make an example of you, so no one will dare to cross me again.

Rising to my full height, I glare down at her. "You better enjoy the next five days. Life, as you know it, is about to end."

Chapter 18

Kingsley

"Yeah, I'm going to be honest," I say as I watch Mason leave, "it feels like I've entered the twilight zone."

Shaking off Mason's weird behavior, I look for Preston, and when my eyes fall on him, I say, "I haven't seen you since the party. Where have you been hiding?"

"I've been helping Falcon," he says, a proud look on his face.

"Oh, are you both Lake and Falcon's assistant now?"

"He was never my assistant, to begin with," Lake mumbles under his breath, which has me laughing.

I glance at Falcon and see him smiling at Preston, then he explains, "Preston is helping me with the business plans for the new company."

"Wow, good for you, Preston."

"I'm just grateful for the opportunity," he brushes off the compliment.

I tilt my head, and ask, "How did you know I was in the pool?"

Preston's face sets into a scowl, as he begins to give me a play by play of the entire night's events.

When he gets to the part where Mason gave me CPR, my hand shoots up. "Wait a second. Rewind, and repeat the part about Mason again."

"He pulled you out and started giving you CPR." Preston's face softens. "I was exhausted just from keeping your head above the water for a minute or so, but Mason kept doing compressions until Layla had to pull him away." He shakes his head with a perplexed look. "It's still hard to believe Serena did that to you."

I don't even take in his last sentence because I'm still stuck on the fact that Mason gave me CPR. Worrying that this incident might have brought Mason's past trauma back to the surface, I turn my gaze to Lake, and ask, "Is Mason okay?"

Lake shakes his head, "What do you mean?"

"Did this incident bring back memories, like with the avalanche?"

"No." Falcon answers. "He didn't mention it at all."

"That's good," I muse.

It also makes me realize that Mason's change in behavior toward me is probably because I almost died.

———————————————

After everyone left, Layla came back wearing her pj's. With the lights dimmed, we sit on the floor, out on the balcony and stare at the stars.

"How do you really feel?" she asks, not taking her gaze off the heavens.

I let out a burst of silent laughter. "You don't believe me when I say I'm okay?"

She turns her head to me. "Not after what happened to me with Grayson. I know you're not okay."

"Yeah," I whisper. "It's weird. One minute I'm totally fine, and the next, it feels as if I'm struggling to breathe. Literally. It's hard to accept the fact that I was almost killed."

"Killed," Layla murmurs. "It sounds like such a small word. It doesn't give the definition of what really happened."

"No, it doesn't."

She reaches over to me and taking my hand, she links our fingers. "Give me your definition."

"I only remember the panic. It's weird," I let out a shaky breath before I continue, "when the avalanche hit me, I didn't feel nearly as panicked as when –" my voice breaks as the desolate feeling creeps back into my heart. "It's hard to put into words. I felt horribly vulnerable and alone. Knowing there was no one to help me, and I couldn't keep my head above the water. I never want to feel that kind of panic again."

Letting go of my hand, Layla scoots closer to me and pulls me into her arms.

After a while, she whispers, "The day you sat down next to me and introduced yourself was one of the best things that ever happened to me. I love you, Kingsley."

"Love you, too," I whisper.

We only watched one episode of *Grace & Frankie* on my laptop before Layla fell asleep.

Leaving the bedroom, I softly shut the door behind me and go sit on the couch. I bring my legs up and hug them to my chest.

It feels like my world has been tainted, as if someone took black paint and splattered it all over my emotions and my beliefs.

A knock at the door pulls me out of my somber thoughts. I get up and go to open it, thinking it's probably Falcon looking for Layla. When I open the door and see Mason, something shifts in my chest.

Mason did CPR on me until emergency services came.

He was literally my heartbeat.

The thought is overwhelming and makes tears push up my throat.

"Did I wake you?" he asks.

I shake my head and step aside so he can come in.

"Why are you sitting in the dark?" he asks.

I close the door before I answer, "Layla just fell asleep, and I came out here so I wouldn't wake her."

"You can't sleep?" he asks, taking a step closer to me.

I shake my head, trying to swallow the emotions down as a tear escapes.

"Babe?" He lifts his hand to my cheek and brushes the tear away. "Come here." He wraps his arms around me and holds me tightly to his chest.

Never in a ka-zillion years would I have thought I'd be crying my heart out in Mason Chargill's arms.

When a sob escapes, he bends down and placing an arm beneath my knees, he picks me up. I wrap my arms around his neck and bury my face against his shoulder as he walks to the couch. He sits down with me on his lap and places a hand behind my head.

After a while, I manage to calm down enough to lift my head and say, "Thank you for giving me CPR."

He doesn't say anything but instead presses a kiss to my forehead. I meet his eyes and wonder who Mason really is. Is he the volatile bad boy or this caring man?

"What's going on in that pretty head of yours?" he whispers.

I've never been one to beat around the bush, so I answer him honestly. "I'm wondering which Mason is the real one; the hotheaded, take-no-prisoners guy, or the kind one."

"Who says I can't be both?" A smile forms around my lips, and then he continues, "I'm ruthless when someone crosses me, but when it comes to my friends and family, I'm protective."

"Well, then I'm glad I'm a friend," I tease.

I begin to pull back so I can get off his lap, but he places a hand on my back, stopping me.

My eyes dart back to his face, and when I see the corner of his mouth lifting, I ask, "I'm a friend, aren't I?"

He remains quiet for a while before he says, "You're a friend... for now."

And that means?

"Are you planning on fighting with me again?"

He shakes his head and a sexy smirk forms around his mouth. "You don't want to know what I'm planning."

I pull a face and grumble, "At least give me time to get back to my old self so I can fight back."

He moves his hand from my back to the side of my neck, and when his thumb brushes over my jaw, a thought begins to niggle in the back of my mind.

As farfetched as it sounds, I have to wonder whether Mason likes me or whether he just feels pity for me because I almost died.

He begins to lean closer to me, his eyes never leaving mine, and then he stops an inch from my face, watching for my reaction before he presses his mouth to mine.

The kiss is soft and quick, but it packs one hell of a punch I didn't expect.

"I'm going to leave you with that thought," he says as he lifts me off his lap and sets me down on the couch. "Get some sleep, Babe."

Wide-eyed, I watch him leave.

Well, that's something I didn't expect.

Angry sex, yes. But... gentle and caring?

I'm not imagining things, right?

Chapter 19

Kingsley

I've been staring at Layla for the last thirty minutes, waiting for her to wake up.

When I can't hold out any longer, I shake her shoulder. "I need you to wake up."

She grumbles something, only stirring.

"Layla, wake up! I need you," I whine, shaking her again.

Her eyes pop open, and she darts up, instantly going into panic mode. "Are you okay? Did something happen?"

I nod and pouting, I mumble, "I'm confused."

Layla blinks then rubs her eyes. "So, you're okay?"

"Far from. I can't make sense of any of it."

"Coffee first," she groans, then falls back against the pillows.

"Coming right up." I dart off the bed and not even bothering to brush my hair, I race to the elevator so I can go get us some coffee.

When the doors open, I freeze, and my eyes widen. Mason's leaning against the back panel and his head lifts slowly from where he was staring at the floor.

When he sees me, the stupid sexy smirk begins to pull at the corner of his mouth. "Did your hair straightener break, or are you going with the all-natural look today?"

"Huh?" I pat the top of my head, then remember it must look like one hell of a mess. Glaring at him, I mumble, "I haven't had coffee yet. Don't mess with me while I'm caffeine-deprived."

I step inside and press the button for the doors to close.

"And just when I think it couldn't look worse, I get to see it from behind," he chuckles.

"Dude," I growl, willing the elevator to move faster.

"I might love your morning look, but for the sake of the other students, let's get this on you."

I glance over my shoulder, ready to snap at him when my eyes bulge as I watch him drag his hoody over his head. The doors ping open, and all I can do is stare at his abs as his t-shirt lifts up for a moment.

Yeah, I love your morning look, as well.

"When you're done drooling, catch the doors before they close," he grumbles as he straightens his shirt covering the strip of golden delicious skin.

I begin to blink and feeling my face heat with embarrassment, I rush forward. I bump into the doors as they start to close, and growling, I smack the metal, "Stupid damn doors!"

I'm almost jogging in my hurry to get away from Mason's gorgeously smirking face, but he grabs hold of my arm and pulls me to a stop. Coming to stand in front of me, he shoves the hoodie over my head, then grumbles, "Left arm." I shove my arm through the sleeve while shooting him a glare. "Right arm." I roll my eyes but do it anyway.

Then he steps right into my personal space as he adjusts the hoodie over all my hair. Holding onto the sides of the fabric, he leans in and presses a kiss to my forehead.

"Go get your coffee, Babe." Not needing to be told twice, I dart around him, and almost fall face down from shock when he slaps my ass.

I let out a squeak before I give him a what-the-fuck scowl. There's a fluttering in my stomach, and I try to ignore it as I dart out of the building.

He's only screwing with you, Kingsley.

Not yet fully recovered from the near-drowning, it feels like I've run a marathon when I reach the café on campus.

The barista smiles at me, but her friendly expression freezes when I say, "Please tell me I can get alcohol with my coffee.

She keeps staring at me as if I've lost my mind, which has me mumbling, "Two coffees and two caffè mochas."

With the order in my hands, I keep glancing around to make sure I don't run into Mason again while I rush back to the dorm. When I reach my suite without anything else happening, I let out a sigh of relief.

"Layla, coffee is here," I call out.

She comes out of the room and sitting down on the couch, she takes one of the cups, and looking at the label, she puts it back down and reaches for the other, "Nourishment before dessert."

I wait for her to take a sip, then say, "Please tell me you know what's going on with Mason."

She immediately smiles widely and wiggles her eyebrows at me as she keeps sipping her coffee. After a couple of seconds, she asks, "He's friendly all of a sudden, right?"

"Yeah, it's creeping me out."

"He's touching you more, right?"

"He slapped my freaking ass this morning," I call out, not even sure how to process it.

"Oooh," she leans forward, "Did you like it?"

"Huh?" I begin to shake my head but then stop, because, with the shock set aside, it did make something flutter inside of me. "Yeah, I suppose I did."

She leans back, and grinning, she mumbles, "Didn't take him for an ass man."

Pinching the fabric of his hoodie between my thumb and forefinger, I pull it away from my chest. "I'm wearing his hoodie. The guy dressed me in the lobby."

Layla keeps drinking the damn beverage, her eyes filled with laughter.

"You're not helping," I grumble as I reach for my own coffee.

I take a huge sip of the warm liquid, hoping it will clear my mind, and then Layla asks, "Is it so hard to believe Mason likes you?"

I tilt my head as I stare at her, and after a while, I begin to nod. "Yes."

"Why?"

"For starters, I'm not his type."

She lifts an eyebrow at me.

"We bicker," I state, "Like... all the time."

195

Her smile widens, and she gestures with her hand for me to go on.

"What more do you want? He picks on me every chance he gets. He's always growling. Damn, even the sex was angry."

Layla sets her empty cup down and reaches for the caffè mocha. "You still need to tell me about the epic sex you had." Sitting back again, she asks, "When last did the two of you bicker?"

I think about the question, and when I can't remember, I shrug.

"Okay, let's be serious," Layla says, and she begins to tick off on her fingers, "You and Mason used to take digs at each other, then you had sex, then you were awkward, then you almost died."

"That pretty much sums it up," I agree.

A serious look tightens Layla's features. "Kingsley, Mason watched you almost die. I think the shock made him realize he cares about you. He never left your side while we were waiting for you to wake up."

I let her words sink in before I admit, "The thought never even crossed my mind. I was just worried I might've triggered his past trauma again." Then I frown, "But I'm not his type."

"Stop saying that," she scolds me. "You're freaking badass, and Mason will be lucky if he ever gets to date you."

Grinning, I chuckle, "Yeah, I am pretty badass."

"Honestly, I think Mason fell for you because you don't take his shit. He would never be happy with some docile airhead."

Wow, she's right.

"Kingsley, you're exactly Mason's type."

For a while, I process everything I've just discovered, then I whisper, "What do I do now?"

"That's the easy part," Layla states as she continues to drink her beverage. "You either tell him you're not interested or you enjoy the ride... literally."

A burst of laughter explodes from me. "And the previous ride was so damn hot."

"Yeah?" Layla shoots up and comes to sit next to me, "Give me the details."

Grinning, I say, "One second we were arguing and the next he had me shoved up against the wall."

"Hot, damn."

Her excitement is infectious, and soon she has me rambling, "The way he kisses. Holy hotness. It felt like he was trying to devour me." I wave a hand over my face as it

197

begins to heat up. "Let's just say, the man knows how to satisfy a girl."

We laugh, and after the excitement dies down, Layla asks, "Do you like Mason?"

"I like him, but…" I pause and try to think of the right words to express my concern. "He's Mason Chargill, the future president of CRC."

"So?" Layla shrugs.

"He's intense, Layla. Liking him won't matter for shit if I can't keep up with his pace."

"Are you afraid he'll grow bored with you?" Trust my friend to be brutally honest.

"That, and what if we give a relationship a chance, and I have to change to fit into his world?" I look down at my hands where they're gripping his sweater. "I like who I am."

"Maybe you should talk to Mason about that. Hear what he actually expects from a relationship before you start worrying. His answer might surprise you." When I just nod, Layla reminds me, "Look at Falcon and me. I didn't change who I am for him, because he loves me for who I am. If I were to change, I'd lose him."

"I know you're right, but I can't help worrying," I admit.

Layla reaches over and gives my hand a squeeze. "Don't think about it too much. If things don't work out between the two of you, at least enjoy the flirting."

Bringing a smile to my face, I agree, "Yeah, I'm totally overthinking things. Besides, it's not every day a girl has a man like Mason giving her attention." Then my smile turns into a mischievous grin. "Can you imagine how confused he would be if I flirted back?"

"I'd pay to see that," Layla laughs.

Feeling better after talking things out with Layla, I get up. "I'm going to shower and get ready for the day." As I walk to the bedroom, I chuckle. "Might even wear something sexy and put on some makeup."

"Yes! Bring out the big guns." Layla rushes after me. "Seeing as he's an ass man, do you have any hot shorts?"

Chapter 20

Mason

Heading to class, Lake slaps a hand against my chest. "You're in trouble."

"Why?" I frown and looking at him, I see him staring at something ahead.

My eyes follow his line of sight, and then my steps falter to a stop, and I growl, "Fuck, I'm so fucking fucked."

Kingsley and Layla are at the end of the hallway, walking toward us. The sight is seriously badass as I watch students give way to them. Guys turn to watch them pass by, and it makes my eyebrow slowly rise.

"Hunt!" I shout from the other side of the hallway. "What the fuck are you wearing?"

Her lips curve into one hell of a seductive grin, which has a direct link to my dick. My eyes slowly sweep over her, and I take in the fucking skimpy shorts that barely cover her important parts.

The parts I don't want another dick seeing.

The boots only make her outfit off the charts hot.

She's wearing a loose sweater which hangs off her left shoulder, and she's straightened her hair. Gone is the rat's nest from this morning.

When she gets close to me, my eyes move up to her face and stop on her glossy mouth. When my eyes lock on hers, I have to suppress the urge to wipe the smokey eyeshadow off with my bare hands.

Her smirk stretches. "They're called clothes, Mason."

I begin to shake my head and grabbing hold of her hip, I yank her right against my chest.

I hear a wave of murmurs ripple through the students around us as they watch Kingsley and me.

Usually, I'd just text the girl to meet me somewhere. I've never been seen publicly with any of them, nevermind flirting with one.

But Kingsley's not just another fuck buddy.

She's so much more.

Leaning down until I can see the dark blue line around her irises clearly, I grumble, "I'm dead sure the panties I ripped off you had more fabric than the shorts you're wearing now. How does it even cover your underwear?"

She places a hand on my shoulder and standing on her toes, her breath skims over my jaw as she stretches to reach my ear. "Who says I'm wearing any?"

The image of her walking around without any underwear on has my dick hardening at record speed.

Before I can think of a way to respond, she moves past me and slaps me on the ass, while sassing me, "Seeing as you have a thing for my ass, you should enjoy watching me walk away."

"She's back to her old self," Lake mutters while chuckling. "I get a feeling you're going to need all the luck you can get."

I turn and watch her sway her fuckable ass all the way down the hallway. "Fuck luck." A satisfied grin forms around my mouth. "My girl is back."

"Speaking of girls," Lake says as we begin to walk again. "Mine's arriving next Saturday."

"Yeah?" I throw my arm around his shoulder. "Are you excited?"

He nods, and I don't miss the look of worry crossing over his features.

"She's going to love you, Lake. It will be impossible for her not to," I encourage him.

"I hope you're right," he murmurs right before we split up to head into our classes.

After class, I walk to my car, where Preston's already waiting for me.

"Do you have everything?" I ask as I press the button for my Bugatti.

Preston nods as he gets into the car.

Glancing at him, I warn, "We're breaking the law, so if you want out, now's the time."

He shakes his head. "I'm all in."

After Preston saved Kingsley, I approached him with my plan. I tested him first, to see if he could be trusted, by asking him to hack into Senator Weinstock's home computer, and he passed with flying colors.

Falcon noticed Preston first, and he was right, the guy has a brilliant mind.

"If shit goes wrong, you stick to the claim that I forced you. Let me take the full brunt of it," I remind him.

"Okay," he nods, then he adds, "They won't be able to track us because I've set up dummy servers all over the world, and I'll be leaving behind an '*Anonymous*' calling card to throw the authorities off our scent."

"Anonymous?" I ask, not quite understanding what he's talking about.

"They're a worldwide hacktivist group."

"Right," I nod as I start the engine and pull out of the parking area. "Keep up the good work, and you might just become my assistant when I get inaugurated as president at CRC."

He begins to blink, then sputters, "Holy cow."

"Did you get the Senator's schedule?" I ask.

"Yes!" His voice brims with excitement while he gives me a quick rundown of the schedule for the rally where Senator Weinstock will be addressing his supporters.

When we walk back into the suite after scouting the location, Preston walks to Falcon's room and knocks on the door.

Falcon opens and seeing it's Preston, he glances to where I am. "Did everything go well?"

"Yeah, we're ready for Tuesday," I answer as I sit down on the couch, pulling my phone out of my pocket. "I even sent my RSVP on behalf of CRC."

"That's good to hear," Falcon says, then he gestures for Preston to walk into the room. "Let's get back to work." Before he closes the door, he looks at me. "Check your email. There's a board meeting announcement for the end of February. I've instructed them to add the proposal to the agenda."

"Will you be ready to present the proposal by then?" I ask while I open my emails.

"Yes, with Preston's help, we'll be ready way before then."

"Good," I mumble as I read over the current agenda for the meeting. Not seeing anything out of the ordinary, I bring up Serena's number and send her a message.

Do you hear that sound?

She reads it within seconds and types out a reply.

What sound?

I smirk and wait a couple of seconds before I text her again.

The sound of the clock ticking...

I wait again, then text her the final message before I close the app.

Tick. Tock. Time's running out for you.

When a message from her comes through, I clear it from my screen without bothering to read it. My phone begins to ring, and it has me grinning with sadistic satisfaction. I watch her name flash on the screen until it goes to voicemail.

That's right, Serena. Panic.

Lake comes out of his room and stretches as he yawns. "Have you had lunch yet?" he asks.

"No, you want to go grab something?"

"Yeah."

We leave the suite and walk to the restaurant on campus.

"We need to do something about the menu," I complain. "I'm not going to survive another four months with the current one."

"I'll check what we can add," Lake says, instantly awake after being drowsy from the nap he just took.

I let out a chuckle. "You should forget about the coffee business and start a chain of restaurants."

He sighs heavily. "I thought about doing that, but I'd eat all my profits."

A burst of laughter escapes as I pat him on the back. "That's for fucking sure."

When we enter the restaurant, my eyes scan over the students until they land on a table where Kingsley and Layla are sharing a huge piece of chocolate cake.

Lake's heading toward our usual table, so I grab hold of his arm and tug him toward them.

"Ladies," I say as I pull out the chair next to Kingsley.

She pops a bite of cake into her mouth as she glances at me.

Da-yumn, I wish my dick was that fork.

Then she sucks the icing off the fucking silverware.

Placing a hand on the table, and the other on the back of her chair, I lean closer. Letting my lips lightly brush across her jaw, I blow a hot breath over her ear. "You keep sucking that fork like a fucking pro, and I'm going to throw you over my shoulder, take you back to your suite, and fuck you senseless."

She begins to cough and drops the fork. Moving my hand to her back, I pat her a couple of times, and when she catches her breath, I whisper again, "Probably the same response you'll have when I thrust my cock into your fuckable mouth."

She makes a squeaking sound and darts up from her chair.

"Need water," she stammers as she rushes away from the table.

"Kingsley," Layla calls out, "there's a whole bottle on the table." Then she laughs and shakes her head at me. "Don't be mean to my friend."

Schooling my face into an innocent look, or as close as I can get to one, I hold up my hands and say, "I didn't do anything."

"Yeah, right," Lake mumbles as he gestures for a waiter. When I get up, he asks, "Are you coming back?"

"Yeah, order for me. If I'm not back by the time you're done, just grab it to go."

I set after Kingsley, and when I walk out of the restaurant, I see her heading toward the dorms.

Glancing to my left, my eyes meet West's. He smirks, then calls out, "Kingsley! Wait up. I want to ask you something."

My eye begins to fucking twitch when he jogs toward her.

Now, the fucker is looking to be killed.

Chapter 21

Kingsley

The smile I had from my encounter with Mason, fades from my face as I glance to where West is jogging toward me. I haven't forgotten what he said to Mason last time they had a fight. I cross my arms as I turn to face him.

When he reaches me, he smirks. "I heard you drowned."

"Near-drowning," I bite out.

"I also heard your heart stopped." There's a flash of smugness on his face.

Slowly, a smile begins to form around my mouth.

I dare you, West.

"So, while you were dead, did you get to see Mason's sister?"

This guy is so twisted, I knew he was going to say something like that the second he mentioned the drowning.

Placing my hand on his shoulder, I take a step closer to him and whisper, "West."

"Yeah?" The smug look only growing in his eyes.

I bring my knee up as hard as I can, hitting him where it hurts most. He sinks to his knees and cups his groin while letting out a pain-filled groan.

I cringe as pain shudders through my knee.

Shit, it always looks so easy.

Ignoring the slight ache, I finish my sentence, "Next time you mess with Mason, you're going to have three Adam's apples."

Bending over, I catch his tearing eyes. "Unless you want children, you won't push me."

When someone presses up against my butt and hands grip my waist, I let out a shriek as I snap up, my back colliding with a solid chest.

"Don't bend over like that with those shorts," Mason's voice rumbles in my ear. He nudges me forward with his body, so I'll start walking, then falls in next to me as he places his arm around my shoulders.

Concerned that I might've overstepped the boundaries by standing up for Mason begins to niggle at the back of my mind. By the time we reach the elevators, it's full-blown worry, which has me nibbling at my bottom lip.

The doors open, and he pushes me inside.

Turning to face him, I begin to ramble, "I'm sorry if I overstepped. It's just –"

When he grabs hold of my butt and lifts me up against his body, my rambling ends with a squeak.

Not wanting to fall, I quickly wrap my legs around his waist and grab hold of his shoulders.

My startled gaze meets his simmering eyes, and I have to swallow hard because the look he's giving me is making heat crash over my body.

His voice is low and gravelly when he asks, "You stood up for me, Hunt?"

I nod, not able to trust that my voice will sound normal right now.

He stares at me until the elevator opens, and then he stalks to my suite.

"Keycard," he growls.

Reaching behind me, I pull it from my back pocket and swipe for the door to open.

Mason pauses at the door, then says, "If you don't want me to fuck you, then you better tell me now."

Yeah, no chance of that happening.

"Stop wasting time, I have a class in twenty minutes."

His mouth curves into that sexy grin, and it has my hormones doing backflips from delight.

Mason stalks inside and waits for me to slam the door shut before he carries me into my bedroom. Putting his knee on the mattress, he lowers me to my back, then grumbles, "Let go."

I drop my feet to the bed and move my hands down to his biceps. I feel the muscles in his left arm ripple beneath my fingers as he moves his hand to between my legs. Dragging a finger along the edge of my shorts, he says, "You're never wearing these again. I'm fucking throwing them in the trash once I have them off you."

I grin up at him. "That's okay, I have three other pairs I can wear."

Shaking his head, he chuckles, but then a serious look settles on his face. "Are you sure about this?"

"What?" I ask. "Us having sex?"

He shakes his head, and his eyes burn into mine. "Us."

Needing to be sure, so I don't make an idiot of myself, I ask, "Dating?"

He shakes his head again, which has me tilting mine with confusion.

"I don't date, Hunt."

Right.

I knew that, but it still stings. After the talk with Layla, I began to feel excited about the idea of dating Mason.

"If we do this, I need you to commit to me," he says, and for a moment, my mind races to catch up.

"Are you talking about us having a relationship?" I ask, feeling lost as fuck right now. "Because that's the same as dating."

He moves his arm under my back and shifts me up to the middle of the bed before he lies down next to me, resting his head on his palm.

"Let me explain this to you in layman's terms," he says. "We won't be going on a couple of dates and then break up. You'll be seen in public with me, meaning the press will be all over it."

Oh… right. Kinda forgot about that.

He brings his hand to my cheek and lightly brushes his fingers over my skin and into my hair. It's a sweet action, but then he continues, "Usually, the girl would have to sign a NDA which states she can't do anything that would damage my image."

I sit up and scowl down at him. "Are you telling me to change who I am?" Waving a finger in front of his face, I snap, "Because that shit will never happen."

I begin to scoot to the edge of the bed, but he grabs hold of me and yanks me back down. Moving over me, he straddles me, and taking hold of my hands, he presses them against the mattress above my head.

"And you say I'm short-tempered?" He chuckles, which only has me glaring at him.

He repositions his hands so he can keep both of mine pinned above my head with one hand, then he brings the other down to my face and brushes a finger over the frown on my forehead.

I duck my head away and glare up at him. "Stop with the soft touches, Mason. Just say what you need to say and get out."

"What I'm trying to say," he says, lifting an eyebrow at me, which looks a lot like a warning for me to shut up, "is that you'll have to commit yourself to me. Yeah, the NDA covers everything from the girl not having a claim to CRC if we decide to split up a year down the line, but –"

I swear my eyes are going to start twitching with anger if he doesn't stop.

"Get off me," I growl, wishing I could knee him into next week.

"Why are you so upset about signing a document?" he asks, finally getting that I'm about to spit fire.

"Did Falcon make Layla sign anything?" I bite out.

"Falcon's not the president of CRC," he states. His features become tight as he begins to lose his temper as well. "We've only known each other for a couple of months. Would it be such a bad thing if I were to ask you to sign the fucking document because I sure as fuck can't risk CRC?"

I yank hard and manage to free my hands. Shoving him off me, I dart away from the bed and rush to the front door. Before I can open it, Mason's hand slams against it.

Raging with anger, I swing around, and then a slap echoes through the suite.

Chapter 22

Mason

The flat of her hand connects with my jaw, and for a moment I have to close my eyes, so I don't do something seriously stupid.

I feel Kingsley yank against the door, and not thinking, I bend down and throw her over my shoulder.

"Mason!" she shrieks.

I carry her back to the bedroom and drop her on the bed, then go to lock the door and pocket the key so she can't leave the room until we're done talking. I take a couple of deep breaths before I turn around to face her.

"What the hell are you doing?" she hisses at me while she gets off the bed and stalks toward me.

As pissed off as I am, I can't help but notice how fucking beautiful she is when she's angry.

"Can you calm down for one minute and just hear what I'm saying?" I ask, my voice tense with anger.

She turns her face away from me and closes her eyes for a couple of seconds before she brings her blazing gaze back to me. "I am not some business deal. A contract? Have you lost your mind? If you can't trust me, then what the hell is the point of having a relationship with me?"

Fucking hell, how am I going to get her to listen to me?

I take a step toward her, but she quickly moves back and holds her hand up between us. "I swear I will lose my shit if you touch me."

I take another deep breath and let it out slowly.

"Kingsley," I say, not quite sure how I'm going to fix this mess. "You don't understand. I ne –"

"Oh, I understand." She places her hands on her hips and shakes her head at me.

I suck my bottom lip between my teeth to keep from responding in anger.

"Don't do that," she snaps.

"Do what?" I ask, confused.

"Don't do that lip thing. You can't look hot while I'm fighting with you."

I let out a burst of laughter, because fuck, this woman will be the end of me.

The laughter fades away as I lock eyes with her. "I've never had a serious relationship before, and I'm really trying here."

Pain flashes over her face, and sounding disappointed, she whispers, "Mason, if you can't trust me, then you don't know me at all." She moves back and sits down on the bed. "Ugh. This is so hard."

After a while, she gets up again and holds out her hand to me. "Give me the key."

Bringing my hand to my face, I wipe tiredly over my eyes before I say, "Neither of us is leaving this room until we've resolved this."

"Seriously?" She crosses her arms. "It's resolved, Mason. I won't be in a *committed* relationship with a guy who can't trust me."

Before I can open my mouth to tell her she misunderstood about the NDA, she continues, "I have to ask," her voice begins to tremble, and I hate when her eyes start to shine, "Have I ever given you any reason to not trust me? Yes, we've only known each other for a couple of months, but when have I ever done anything to make you doubt my character?"

"Hunt," I say, trying to get her to shut up for a second.

"Have you heard me tell people we slept together?"

"Kingsley, shut up," I snap, just needing a fucking second.

"It really hurts, Mason. I had to trust you with my life twice, and you want me to sign a document?"

"Woman! Shut the fuck up so I can just get a moment to speak!" I shout.

Her eyes widen, but at least she's quiet.

"I never said I want you to sign a fucking NDA."

She begins to blink as if she still doesn't understand what I'm saying.

"Did you hear what I just said?" I let out a frustrated breath. "I was just telling you about the fucking document, but I never said I didn't trust you, and you had to sign it."

"You didn't?" she asks, the anger draining from her face and leaving her with a look of embarrassment. She lifts her shoulders and pulls an awkward face. "Oops."

"Oops?" I let out a heavy breath. "You just lost your shit and oops?"

Kingsley glances down at her hands where she's wringing them, then she whispers, "I'm sorry. I really thought you wanted me to sign the thing."

"Then I would've had you sign it before I fucked you the first time," I remind her.

"True." Her shoulders slump, and she looks downright miserable. "Trust me to ruin the moment."

"Can I touch you now?" I ask to make sure it's safe. "Or are you going to slap me again?"

Looking apologetic, Kingsley does this fucking cute thing with her mouth, where she presses her lips together and glances up at me with huge blue eyes. "I'm sorry I slapped you."

"And you won't do it again."

Her lips begin to lift at the side, but only slightly. "I won't do it again."

When I don't move, she places her hands behind her back and takes two steps closer to me.

"Are you trying to get out of trouble by being cute?" I ask, the corner of my mouth lifting.

She nods, then darts forward and grabbing hold of my sweater, she eagerly looks up. "Is it working?"

I let out a chuckle. "I have to say, I'm surprised by that temper of yours." Moving an arm around her, I press my hand to her lower back so she'll move closer to me. "First, you knee the fucker, and then you let me have it."

Her shoulders slump again.

"I'm sorry," she whispers again.

"How sorry?" I ask, my lips curving into a grin.

"Very." Kingsley glances up at me, and when she sees the grin, relief washes over her face.

"Show me," I whisper.

She places her hands on my shoulders and standing on her toes, she stretches but only manages to press a kiss to my chin.

"Is that it?" I ask, totally taking advantage of the moment.

Kingsley gets a mischievous look, and taking hold of my hand, she pulls me toward the bed. I begin to laugh when she climbs onto the mattress and stands on it. I have to look up at her, and it has her wagging her eyebrows at me.

Lifting her hand to my face, she brushes her fingers over the skin where she slapped me, then leaning down, she presses a kiss to the spot.

I move forward and wrap my arms around her ass, hugging her to me.

Framing my face with her hands, she begins to press kisses all over it. When she reaches my mouth, she stops, and meeting my eyes, she whispers, "Do you still want to be in a relationship with this crazy chick?"

Smiling, I nod. "Your crazy plays well with my crazy."

My words make her smile, and then she skims her mouth over mine. It's soft touches until I need more, and I have to take over.

I lower an arm to her legs and pull them from under her. She lets out a playful shriek as she falls back onto the bed, then she scoots up so I can lie down next to her. I rest my head on my palm and bring my other hand to her face.

Tracing the outline of her mouth, I say, "I like you, Hunt."

Her mouth curves up under my finger. "Yeah? You don't want to strangle me anymore?"

I shake my head.

"I like you, too."

"Yeah? I don't scare you anymore?"

Her smile is filled with warmth that lights up her eyes as she wraps her arms around my neck. "No, how can I be scared of you after you saved my life twice?"

"Maybe I saved you so I could torture you," I tease as I lean down. Lightly biting her bottom lip, I suck it into my mouth before I let it go.

"Yeah?" She wiggles closer to me. "I'm pretty sure I'm going to like whatever torture you have in mind for me."

"Hmm… kinky," I groan.

She pulls back, and her eyes widen. "Hold on. We're not talking about whips and shit, right?"

"Hunt, the only thing touching your ass will be my hand, so don't push it. I will throw you over my knee."

She actually thinks about it, and it has me looking at her with surprise. "You like the idea of me spanking you?"

"Ahh... uhm..." she stammers, her cheeks flushing pink. "I didn't say that."

I brush my mouth teasingly over hers. "Oh, you didn't have to say a word, your reaction was answer enough."

Chapter 23

Kingsley

"I missed my class," I whisper between kisses.

Mason lifts his head and glances at his watch, then shrugs. "I'll help you catch up on the work you're missing."

"Yeah?" I smile at him.

"Yeah."

"Can I ask you a question?" I hope he won't take it the wrong way, but it's something I'm really worried about.

"Sure," he replies, resting his head on his palm again so he can look at me.

Lowering my eyes from his, I reach for his sweater by his abs and begin to fiddle with the fabric. "Are you sure you like me? You don't just feel pity because I almost died?"

When he doesn't say anything, I dart a glance up at him, and seeing the frown on his face, I begin to ramble,

"It's just you really hated me, and then it just suddenly changed. I –"

Mason moves over me, and I have to open my legs to accommodate him. He braces his arms on either side of my head, and tilting his head, he says, "Now that I have your full attention before you start rambling, and I don't get a word in." I glance to the side because I'm feeling anxious about his answer. "I never hated you to begin with."

Slowly, I bring my eyes back to his, and when I see an affectionate look softening his features, I feel a fluttering of hope.

"When we met, I was a mess. I think I liked you from the start, and I just didn't know how to process it."

A slight smile begins to pull at my mouth.

"Kingsley," hearing him say my name makes my heart expand and tingles spread over my body, "seeing you just lie there, with no heartbeat?" He lowers his head and buries his face in my neck. "That was one hell of a wake-up call," he whispers, his breath fanning over my skin.

I lift my arms and wrap them around him, hugging him tightly.

"That's when I realized I needed to see your smile again. I needed to hear you sassing me." He lifts his head, and for a moment, his eyes just drift over my face. "I needed to see your beautiful face again."

A grin widens the slight smile on my face. "You think I'm beautiful?"

"In a very different way than anyone else." He brings a hand to my face and brushes his fingers along the side of my eye and down to my jaw. "There was a moment I thought you were going to die, and it felt like someone ripped the sun right from the sky. Your beauty is bright. It's cheerful and warm, and that's why I struggled to get along with you in the beginning."

I hesitate, not wanting to upset him, but he notices it, and smiling, he says, "Spit it out. I can see you want to say something."

"I overheard you telling Lake that I reminded you of your sister." I pull a face. "Yeah, saying it out loud..." I cringe a little.

To my surprise, he lets out a chuckle. "Babe, you look nothing like Jennifer. She had blonde hair, so I'm more likely to see a resemblance between her and Layla."

I let out a breath of relief. "Thank God."

"She was full of life. She always saw the positive side of everything. Like you, she thought everything was unicorns farting glitter and butterflies shitting all over the flowers."

I crack up, and after a couple of seconds, I tap at his back. "Off... can't... breathe."

When he rolls off me and just watches me laugh with a smile on his face. Taking in his striking features, my laughter fades because there's really not a more attractive man out there.

I sit up and moving onto my knees, I frame his face with my hands. "Do you have any idea how hot you are?"

The sexy smirk pulls at his lips.

Nodding, I grin, "Especially when you smirk like that."

There's a playful glint in his eyes as he bites his bottom lip.

I let out a dreamy sigh, "Now I'm just going to have to jump your bones."

He moves onto his back and pulls me closer, so I'm straddling him. "Yeah?"

I nod as I lean down and press a kiss to his jaw.

"There's one specific bone I'd like for you to focus on," he teases.

"Mmmh..." I brush my mouth down to his neck and letting my tongue dart out, I swirl it in a circle over his pulse.

"That's it. Get naked right now," he growls as he grabs hold of my hips and moves me off of him.

When he reaches for my shorts, I say, "I've got this. Get rid of your own clothes."

Grabbing hold of the hem of my sweater, I pull it over my head.

Mason gets off the bed, and my hands still behind my back, where I'm unclasping my bra.

Watching him drag his sweater and t-shirt off brings a huge smile to my face. I didn't get a good look at him the last time we had sex, so I'm not missing out on this opportunity to stare.

Ripped, golden skin. Freaking paradise.

His movements slow down as he reaches for his pants. I tilt my head, and my tongue darts out, wetting my lips when he moves even slower as he pulls the zipper down.

Happy trail. V line. Hot damn.

My eyes are still glued to the hard lines on his lower abdomen when he steps out of his pants, shoes, and socks.

Darting forward, he shoves me onto my back. "I can see you're a little preoccupied, so I'll just undress you," he teases as he pushes a hand under my back and unclasps my bra. He pulls it off me and throws it to the side.

He yanks my boots off before moving to my shorts. Undoing the button on my shorts, he says, "I was serious. These are going to the trash."

"Which means you'll never see me in them again." I wiggle my eyebrows when he stops to actually think about it.

"Fine, you can wear them, but only for me to see."

I grin because his possessiveness makes me feel special.

He pulls my shorts off and tossing the fabric over his shoulder, his eyes freeze on me. "You were serious?"

I forgot about the not wearing underwear comment earlier.

He tilts his head and snaps his eyes up to mine. "I think I totally underestimated you."

I nod. "That's for sure."

Placing his hands on my hips, his touch moves upward until he cups my breasts.

I lower my eyes to where he's touching me, and I watch as he begins to caress my body as if he's trying to memorize the feel of it.

He leans forward and presses a kiss to my stomach, then another to the swell of my breast over my heart. Lying down on my right, he whispers, "Turn on your side with your back to me."

Okay?

I do as he asks, and he pushes his arm in under my head while pulling me back against his body.

"Are we seriously going to take a nap now?" I ask, but then my eyes widen as his right hand slips around my front, and he cups me between my legs. "Oh…" He presses a kiss to my shoulder, and another beneath my ear before he lightly bites my earlobe. "Ohh…"

He pushes a finger inside me but then pulls it back out only to rub circles around my opening.

"Love how wet you are for me, Hunt."

"So, take the damn plunge already," I growl when he keeps rubbing all around, except for where I want him.

He chuckles and brushes his lips over my neck, then his voice rumbles, "You want me to finger you?"

My breaths come faster, and I have to swallow the urgent need down. "Desperately."

"Mmmh," he hums against my skin. "Not desperate enough."

I move my hands down, but the instant I touch his wrist, he growls, "No, Hunt. Bring your hands up."

"This is torture," I groan.

He chuckles. "Exactly."

Mason

Her body begins to writhe against mine, but I keep the pressure even as I purposely avoid her clit and opening.

"Mace," she gasps, fisting the covers with her left hand while reaching back with her right, and grabbing hold of my hair. "I'm about to reach DEFCON one, and you'll lose your hair," she threatens me.

"So, you're still at level two?" I tease, and then I slightly dip my finger inside of her again.

"Was." She gasps for air and grinds her ass against my cock while she tightens her fist in my hair. "One… crap… definitely one."

My eyes drift over her body, and fuck, it's a breathtaking sight. I push my finger inside her as my eyes return to her parted lips. I watch as the breaths explode from her, and when I flatten my palm against her clit, she arches into me as a moan escapes her.

Her body convulses as the orgasm hits, and I push my finger in as far as I can, then curl it.

"Shit," she gasps, and her body tightens, and she stops breathing for a second, looking like an angel suspended in a moment of ecstasy.

Pulling my hand away, I bring it to my cock and pushing her more onto her stomach, I force her legs open with mine. I press a kiss to her shoulder blade as I position myself at her entrance, and then grab hold of her hip as I thrust inside of her.

She lets out another gasp, tightening her grip on the covers. I pull my arm from under her head and brace myself on my elbow as I pull out, then drive back inside of her.

When she comes down from her orgasm and her ass begins to grind against me again, I move my hand back between her legs and rub her clit, increasing the pressure on it every time I thrust inside her.

"I can't," she whispers breathlessly. "Too intense."

I press a kiss against her shoulder again, then bite her lightly. My hips keep moving, driving into her harder and faster as I feel my own orgasm build.

"Mason," she moans. "I…"

I pinch her clit as I thrust hard into her until my pelvis is flush with her ass. Pleasure rushes over my body, and it forces my hips to move. The sound of our skin connecting mixes with Kingsley's cry as she orgasms again, and the sound makes me slam inside of her until her breaths are nothing but gasps and moans.

My body shudders against her as I empty myself inside her, and only then do I let go of her clit. I bring my hand to her breast, and cupping it, I press breathless kisses over her shoulder and neck while my movements slow down to lazy plunges as we both come down from our highs.

When she finally catches her breath, she says, "I think you broke my vagina."

I begin to laugh and quickly pull out of her. "I'm going to take that as a compliment."

I turn her over onto her back and press a kiss to her mouth. Lifting my head, our eyes meet, and it feels like a tender moment passes between us.

It's something I haven't felt before.

It makes my feelings of protectiveness for this woman spread to my heart. I want to be the only one to hold her, to kiss her, to fuck her.

I've never felt greed before today, not until I realized I don't want to share her smiles with anyone. I don't want to share her.

"What's that look for?" she whispers as she brings her hand to my arm.

She begins to draw random patterns on my shoulder while I search for the right words.

Chapter 24

Kingsley

The sex was mindblowing, but right now, the look on his face has me holding my breath and my heart beating over time.

My hand stills on his shoulder when he remains silent.

"Mace?" I whisper, wondering where his mind is at.

"It's nothing," he says, and I can see the smile is forced as it forms around his mouth.

Needing to use the bathroom, I pull away from him, and I struggle not to squeeze my legs together, but the second I'm in the bathroom, I shut the door and run for the toilet.

I use the moment to think about Mason's weird behavior. The look on his face was something similar to love. Was that only my post-orgasmic bliss imagining things?

I finish up and wash my hands. When I reach for the bathrobe, an apprehensive feeling skitters down my spine.

I pull on the robe and take a deep breath before I open the door. I can't make myself take a step forward when my eyes fall on Mason, where he's dragging his sweater on. When he's done, he picks up my clothes from the floor and set them down on the bed, and then only does he look at me.

Déjà vu is a bitch.

I try to stay calm as I say, "I'll let you out." Darting past him, I stop at the locked door and close my eyes for a second before I force a burst of laughter over my lips. "You have the key."

"Lucky for me," he says. He comes up behind me and taking hold of my shoulders, he turns me around. "You think I'm going to make a run for it?"

Okay, this is not playing out according to the script.

I let out a nervous chuckle and admit, "I have no idea what you planned to do."

Taking hold of the back of my neck, he pulls me to his chest. He presses a kiss to the top of my head just like he did the last time we slept together.

Before I can pull back, he brings his other hand to my chin and nudges my face up. "Stop overthinking things,

Hunt. I'm not ready to talk about my feelings, so don't take it the wrong way and think I'm pulling away because I'm not." He presses a kiss to my mouth, then grumbles, "Get your ass dressed, and let's go grab some food."

I walk to my closet and grab a pair of jeans and a long-sleeve shirt. Holding the clothes in my hands, I turn back to Mason. "I'm sorry I keep misreading things."

"I understand," he answers, and sitting down on the edge of the bed, he continues, "Once you know me better, things will get easier."

I nod because he's right. I place the clothes on the side of the bed then rummage through my drawers for underwear. "What's your favorite color?"

"Black."

I let out a huff of laughter, then I tease him, "I should've known." I turn around with a pair of matching black lace underwear.

"Oh, wait. In that case, I don't have a favorite color. We can go with translucent."

I begin to laugh as I drag my panties on and almost losing my balance, I quickly brace my hand on the bed.

"Is it weird that I love your clumsiness?" Mason asks as he gets up, and crouching in front of me, he takes hold of my panties and pulls them up my legs. He presses a kiss to my hip, and it makes me feel treasured.

I stand with a grin as he picks up my bra and leaning into me, he clips it on then he holds the straps open for me. "Arms." I push them through the loops then burst out laughing when he adjusts the girls in the cups.

Shooting me a smile, he grabs my jeans, and when he has me fully dressed, he leans in and presses a kiss to mouth. Taking my hand, he says, "Let's go eat."

When we get into the elevator, he brings his free hand up to my hair and combs his fingers through the strands. "You had a couple sticking up."

"I wonder why?" I wink at him, and it brings the sexy grin back to his face.

When we walk out of the dorm, I press my cheek to his arm and smile up at him. "I like this."

"Yeah?" He lets go of my hand and places his arm around my shoulder, pulling me to his side. "I like it too."

Mason

When Tuesday comes, it feels like I'm on a high.

I get dressed in a suit but skip the tie. Looking at myself in the mirror, I make sure I look every bit the part of the future president of CRC.

When I walk out into the living room, the corner of Falcon's mouth lifts. "Dressed to kill?"

"You've got that right."

Lake comes out, struggling with his tie again. "Mace, help."

I walk over to him and fix his tie, then pat him on the shoulder. "Good to go."

"Thanks, buddy."

There's a knock at the door, and Falcon opens it. Preston clears his throat, his eyes on the screen of his phone. "I'm all set. The servers are pinging all over the place."

"I feel I should warn you," Lake says as he walks toward Preston. He places his arm around his shoulders, then gestures to Falcon and me. "If you make yourself irreplaceable, they will never let you go. You still have time to save yourself, unlike me." Lake pulls dramatically away from Preston. "Run, Preston. Save yourself."

Falcon begins to chuckle, and I can only shake my head while I smile at them.

Preston still has to work on his sense of humor, because he's dead serious when he says, "No, thank you. I'm hoping that will happen."

"Why?" I ask, taking a couple of steps closer to him.

Preston looks down at his phone, then tucks it into his pocket. His face flushes red before he answers, "I don't want to be known as a nerd or just another paper pusher who happens to have a brain."

I cross my arms and feel Falcon move closer until he's standing next to me.

"I want to make something of myself. You know? I want to be more."

"And you think working with us will give you that?" Falcon asks.

Preston shakes his head, and then he glances at me before looking at Falcon. "I don't *think* so. I *know* working with you will make it happen."

Falcon moves first and goes to stand in front of Preston. He holds his hand out to him, and when they shake, he says, "Then I look forward to creating the future with you."

Preston's face lights up. "So, I won't just be working on the business plan with you?"

Falcon shakes his head and smiles, "No, you're going to help me bring ideas to fruition. When the business plan is completed, we'll begin looking at patents we can purchase."

"Holy cow, that's going to be awesome," Preston almost gushes.

"Let's get going, guys," I say.

When we walk out of the building, Falcon walks ahead, with Lake right behind him. I'm last, and as my eyes scan over the grounds, I notice how students stop to watch as we head to our cars.

Preston falls in next to me, and whispering, he asks, "Why do you always walk like this and not next to each other?"

Smirking at him, I say, "Falcon protects Lake."

"And you?"

I throw my arm around Preston's shoulders. "I make sure no one stabs them in the back."

"Right." The words sink in, and with wide eyes, he sputters, "I-I'll n-never do t-that."

Patting him on the back, I chuckle, "I'm just fucking with you."

Chapter 25

Mason

"As a firm supporter," Senator Weinstock pauses and jabs his forefinger at the podium, "CRC Holdings have backed me every step of the way. They have provided the much-needed funds to help create jobs." His eyes scan over the ocean of people who are here to support him. "And today, more small businesses have been able to keep their doors open over the past six months, due to the support of CRC Holdings."

Glancing to the Senator's left, I watch Serena smiling brightly where she's standing next to her mother.

My phone begins to ring, and I step to the side before I answer, "Chargill."

"Are you all set?" Julian asks. "Do you need me to come down to the rally?"

"No, we have everything covered. Trust me to handle this."

I went to meet with Julian when I popped into the office. He agreed to let me take his place after I showed him the proposal Dad had me look at. Lucky for me, it was from the Senator, and how he planned to expand the harbor. Also lucky for me, Preston hacked into the Senator's home computer, where we stumbled across his real plans. He would pocket half the investment from CRC. So, it's with a clear conscience that I'm ruining the Senator's career.

"I trust you." I hear Julian take a deep breath, and then he says, "We should have dinner, Mason."

"We can meet up next week."

"That sounds great." He lets out a relieved sigh, and it makes me feel like shit for putting a distance between us after Jen's death. There's a moment's pause, then he adds, "Remember, make sure CRC comes through this unscathed."

"I've got this."

"Good luck."

I end the call and walk back to where Falcon and Lake are.

Pressing on my ear, I ask, "Preston, are we good to go?"

All four of us have earpieces so we can communicate easily.

"Yes, you remember the signal, right?" his reply comes through the earpiece.

"I adjust my cufflink."

"Break a leg," he says, then he begins to sputter, "I-I don't m-mean literally."

Lake pats me on the shoulder and says, "I'm going to head to the rendezvous point, so I'm near Preston if anything goes wrong."

"You do that."

I turn to Falcon, and when our eyes meet, he says, "Go do this for our women."

I nod and squaring my shoulders, I grumble, "Time to make my debut."

A stage assistant comes over to me and attaches a microphone to my jacket.

"You're good to go," she says as she steps back.

The Senator begins to introduce me, which has me fisting my hands at my sides.

"Mason Chargill is a bright young man, born and bred right here in California. Today he represents CRC Holdings as the future president, and it is my great pleasure to welcome him to the stage."

One hell of a loud applause breaks out, and when I walk out onto the stage, it grows even louder.

I take Senator Weinstock's outstretched hand and shake it. He leans closer and says, "I'm sorry to hear Julian's under the weather, but we're honored to have you."

"Thank you, Senator."

It took me eight days to plan this moment, and now that I'm here, it makes me feel a sense of power I haven't felt before. My heart is racing in my chest as my eyes scan over the ocean of people.

Cameras move in front of the stage, and for a moment, my stomach turns with nerves from being on live television.

When silence falls over the crowd, I raise my chin and square my shoulders. Placing my hands on either side of the podium, I wait for a pregnant pause to build before I say, "Thank you for having me, Senator Weinstock."

I clear my throat and begin with the fake speech, so I'll sound like I'm here for CRC and not revenge. "We grow great by dreams. All big men are dreamers. They see things in the soft haze of a spring day or in the red fire of a long winter's evening." I swallow, and my eyes lock with the camera in front of me. "Some of us let these dreams die, but others nourish and protect them; nurse them through bad days till they bring them to the sunshine and light which comes always to those who sincerely hope that their dreams will come true." Taking a deep breath, I lift my hands from the podium and take a step backward. "Words spoken by Woodrow Wilson."

Applause breaks out, and I wait for it to die down.

Fuck, there's so many people.

I take another deep breath, then I continue, "During my attendance at Trinity Academy, I had the great pleasure of meeting two students who brought sunshine and light to our campus. Like any other student, they hope their dreams will come true. We at CRC Holdings invest to help bring those dreams to realization."

Another applause engulfs the area.

It's showtime.

My stomach feels like it's twisted in knots while my heart keeps racing as if I'm running a fucking marathon.

I wait for the applause and cheers from the crowd to calm down before I bring my hands up as if I'm going to adjust the collar of my suit jacket, and taking a deep breath, I adjust my cufflink.

This is for you, Hunt.

Within seconds all the screens around the LA Memorial Coliseum blacks out. Static noise fills the air, and then manic laughter sounds up.

"What's happening?" I ask, hoping to God I'm pulling off the surprise act.

"And your microphone is cut," Preston says through the earpiece. "I will tell you before I turn it back on."

I nod, knowing he can see me.

A murmur of confused voices spread through the crowd.

"*Time to pay the piper, bitch*," comes over the speakers. Preston electronically altered my voice for the intro.

"What's this?" Senator Weinstock asks.

"Daddy," Serena anxiously cries. "Make it stop. Quickly!" Panic settles over her face as she looks at me.

I walk over to her and place my arm around her shoulder, so it gives the crowd and cameras the impression that I'm supportive of Serena.

"Please don't do this," she hisses.

Leaning closer to her, I whisper, "I fucking warned you, Serena. You fucked with the wrong man."

The footage I took from the Thanksgiving function pops up on the screen. I fake another surprised look, while I remember how hard Preston worked to blur out all the faces. Except for one, of course. He also had to go through months of footage to compile voice clips of Serena talking so we could play them while the video showed.

The video up on the screens shows Serena walking with the pie behind the lining of tables, and then her voice sounds up, "*You degraded me and offended my parents in front of the entire nation.*" Serena waits until Layla gets closer, and then only does she step up to the table, holding the pie out to Layla.

"Oh, God!" Serena whimpers. "I can't believe you're taking this so far."

I turn my head to her and growl, "I'll never forget Falcon's face while they were treating Layla. Honestly, if I could kill you, I would. Unfortunately, I can't, so I have to settle for this."

"Shut it down!" Senator Weinstock yells, when it's clear they can't bypass Preston to take back control of the system.

Then Serena's voice echoes loudly from the speakers, "*You made a big mistake.*" The image switches to Layla collapsing and being rushed out of the room. "*You made a big mistake.*"

The screen blacks out again, and Senator Weinstock's voice returns to the speakers, "Shut it off!"

"Mason!" Serena screams as she turns to me, fear tightening her face.

My eyes meet hers with a glacial stare before I look back to the screen. "We're not done yet."

The footage from the indoor pool begins to play, and my heart painfully constricts as it shows Kingsley's near-drowning. Her face has also been blurred out, but not Serena's.

There's chaos on stage as people rush around to try to stop the footage from being broadcasted on live television, but the cameramen keep airing.

"*I had them eating out of the palm of my hand,*" Serena's voice sneers, and then the scene plays out where she pushes Kingsley into the pool.

Seeing it again doesn't make the blow of pain any lighter, and I bring my hand up, shoving my fingers through my hair as I watch Kingsley go under. She only comes up once before she sinks again.

I turn away from the screen, facing Serena because I know what's coming next, and I want to see her expression as she watches Kingsley's body stop fighting for air. The only time I watched it, it left me puking my guts out.

Knowing everyone is preoccupied, I take a step closer to Serena and growl, "I had to watch the woman I would die for, gasping for her last breath," When she glances at me, I snap, "Watch the fucking screen." Her eyes dart back to the footage, and she lifts a trembling hand to cover her mouth. "Her heart stopped because of you. To me, you are nothing more than a fucking murderer."

Every bit of anger I've been holding back, every speck of hatred I had to swallow rushes to the surface when I hear Serena's voice come over the speakers again, *"You made a big mistake."*

"I didn't mean for her to drown," Serena sobs, and then her face crumbles as she begins to cry. Suddenly her head snaps up, and a look of desperation flashes in her eyes. "Mrs. Reyes told me to give Layla the pie. I only did as I was told."

What the fuck?

Icy prickles of shock ripples over me.

Surely Mrs. Reyes wouldn't have gone that far?

Would she really hurt her own son like that?

The questions are fleeting before the answer settles hard in my gut.

Yes. Yes, she would.

Needing to make sure Serena isn't lying, I ask, "Do you have proof?"

"Of course." Serena digs in her bag and hands me her phone. "All the texts are on there. Please, Mason. I never meant for it to go that far."

Rage makes it hard for me to speak, as I bite out, "You're getting off light, Serena. If I had my way, you'd be dead. You just saw it for yourself," I gesture to the screen where all the plans the good Senator had for CRC's investment, scrolls over the screen, "accidents happen so easily."

"You're a corrupt bastard," a man shouts from the crowd.

"Thief! That money was meant to better our lives!"

"Down with Weinstock!" another yells, and it catches on until the crowd is chanting, "Down with Weinstock!"

I turn to face Senator Weinstock, who's frozen with shock, his skin almost looking grey from worry.

"Your microphone is active again," Preston's voice sounds up in my ear. "You're good to go."

Leveling the senator with a glare which shows everything I'm feeling, I say, "I am shocked to my core by what I witnessed here today. CRC Holdings will look into this horrifying matter, and if proved to be correct, then CRC Holdings will no longer support Senator Weinstock, and charges will be brought against the Senator and Miss Weinstock."

When I finish, an elderly woman asks, "What happened to those poor girls?"

"She's a murderer!"

"Get them!"

Absolute chaos breaks out in the stadium as people rush the stage. Security quickly surrounds us, escorting us to the back.

I split away from the security team, who's trying to get the Senator and his family to safety and jog over to where Falcon is waiting.

"Let's get Preston and get out of here," I say. "The crowd's going crazy."

"Preston, get your ass to the rendezvous point right now," Lake's voice sounds over the earpieces.

"I'm coming." I hear Preston's breaths as he runs, and then he gasps, "Next time can we pick a place that doesn't have so many stairs?"

"We're running out of time," Lake sings. "Oh, there you are. Move it. Move it. Move it."

"Lake, you're going to give Preston a nervous breakdown," Falcon jokes.

"He knows I'm joking. Right, Preston?"

All we get from Preston is wheezing, which makes me chuckle as I climb into my car. I wait for Falcon to pull out before I fall in behind him.

Minutes later, Falcon says, "We're coming up on the intersection, Lake."

"Are we still good, Preston?" I ask.

"Yes, they haven't narrowed in on us yet."

"Then why the fuck am I hearing sirens?" My heartbeat begins speeding up all over again when I spot the cop cars coming from the opposite direction, but when they speed right past us, I let out a breath of relief.

"Relax," Preston says, "They're heading to the stadium."

"Dude, did you hack the cops as well?" I ask with total disbelief.

"Just to keep an eye on what they were doing," Preston defends himself.

"Fuck," I spit out. "I don't want to end up in federal prison."

"Technically, I'm the hacker," Preston says matter-of-factly."

Lake comes speeding from the right side, turning sharply to squeeze in between Falcon and me, and I have to swerve to the right, so I don't hit him.

"Fuckers! The both of you better run when we get back to campus," I growl.

We drive for a while, and when we take the exit toward Ojai, Preston mournfully says, "She served us well."

"Toss the fucking laptop," I grumble.

"Fly free," Lake yells as Preston throws the wiped laptop, so it shatters against the concrete.

"I believe I can fly," Lake sings. "I believe I can touch the sky."

"Shut up," Falcon, and I yell at the same time.

"People don't appreciate great talent anymore," Lake mumbles. Then he says, "Preston?"

"Yes?"

"Weren't you supposed to wear gloves?"

I feel an actual migraine come on, as I shout, "You just threw your fucking fingerprints out the window!"

"Of course, I wore gloves," Preston says.

"You can do it," Lake whispers, and that's when I realize they're screwing with me.

"He's going to kill me," Preston whispers back, while I glare at the back of Lake's Koenigsegg Regera.

"We're just fucking with you," Preston says, then he quickly adds, "I'm sorry. Please don't hit me when we get back to campus."

Fuck, they really had me there for a moment.

"I swear, if I didn't love my car so much, I'd ram it up the ass of your Regera right now," I spit at Lake.

"Do you like my ass that much?" Lake croons over the earpiece.

Falcon's car swerves slightly as his laughter sounds up, and it has me grinning as well.

Fuckers. All of them.

Chapter 26

Kingsley

Before the guys left, Falcon told us to watch Senator Weinstock's rally because Mason would be standing in for Julian on behalf of CRC.

I carry the candy and popcorn over to the coffee table and say, "I'm a little peeved that Mason didn't tell me anything about this rally." I look down at our stash of snacks and ask, "Do I need to get anything else?"

Layla takes hold of my hand and pulls me down onto the couch. "Sit your butt down. We have enough snacks and drinks."

I snuggle into the one corner and grab a Hershey's bar. I'm just about to take a bite when Layla grabs my hand excitedly, and the chocolate bounces up and down in front of my open mouth. "Look!" She slumps back against the couch. "Falcon looks so sexy in that suit."

My eyes snap to the TV, and a second later, I'm grinning like an idiot, too. Layla's still holding onto my hand, and the chocolate is totally forgotten.

"It's hard to believe," I whisper.

Layla scoots closer to me and rests her head against my shoulder. "That you and Mason are dating?" She scrunches her nose. "You're right, it's hard to believe."

I watch him shake hands with people, his shoulders squared, his toned body exuding power.

"How did it happen, Layla?" I murmur. "How did I get such an amazing man to even look my way?"

Layla sits up and bringing her hand to my face, she tucks a couple of strands behind my ear. "Kingsley, why wouldn't you attract him? You're a powerhouse."

I smile at her. "Aww… I love you, my friend."

She hugs me and then takes hold of my hand and bringing it to her mouth, she takes a bite of my chocolate. She chews and swallows before she says, "Love you, too."

The Senator begins to talk, but my eyes go to Serena, who's standing slightly to the back.

"I've never hated anyone until her," I admit to Layla.

"That makes two of us. I swear she sets off my bitch alarm just by waking up in the morning."

I begin to laugh. "Bitch alarm." I hold my hand up for a high five and slapping it, Layla grins.

The Senator welcomes Mason, and it has me sitting upright. When Mason walks out onto the stage, it feels like everything inside of me flutters, not just my stomach.

When the applause from the audience fades, Mason says, *"Thank you for having me, Senator Weinstock."*

I slap a hand over my heart. "I'm so freaking proud of him." Emotion wells in my chest. "Crap, I'm going to cry."

Layla snuggles up to me again, and taking the chocolate from my hand, she tosses it on the table, and then she links our fingers.

When Mason quotes Woodrow Wilson, it feels like I'm being hit by wave after wave of goosebumps.

"During my attendance at Trinity Academy, I had the great pleasure of meeting two students who brought sunshine and light to our campus. Like any other student, they hope their dreams will come true. We at CRC Holdings invest to help bring those dreams to realization."

"Aaaaahhhhhh!" Layla and I shriek at the same time, bouncing on the couch.

"That's us, right?" I ask, to be sure.

"I'd kick his butt if it's not," she quips.

When Mason adjusts his cufflink, I almost begin to drool. "Please tell me we can rewind so I can see him do that again."

"It will be on YouTube," Layla states.

"True."

Static comes from the TV, which has me frowning, "Is that our TV or a problem on their side?"

Manic laughter sounds up, which has Layla sitting back up. *"Time to pay the piper, bitch."*

"Holy crap," Layla breathes with surprise.

My mouth just hangs open as I stare at the screen.

We watch as panic erupts on stage and how Mason walks over to Serena. I tilt my head and glare at the TV when he places his arm around her shoulder.

He leans closer and says something to her, and then I almost dislocate my jaw as my mouth falls open for a second time. The huge screen on stage shows Serena handing Layla the pie.

Layla turns her head slowly to me and asks, "It wasn't the apple juice?"

"I don't know," I shrug.

Even though Layla's face is blurred out, I still wrap an arm around her when we watch her collapse on screen.

Serena says something, and I see a flash of anger on Mason's face before he turns his back to the camera.

Then Serena's voice echoes loudly from the speakers, *"You made a big mistake."*

"Didn't she say that after you slapped her the day Mason jumped into the pool with me?" I ask.

"I can't even remember."

The screen on stage blacks out, and then Serena screeches like a dying cow. "Wow, so much for being graceful," I say wryly.

Layla's phone rings and she quickly answers when she sees it's Falcon.

"What are you guys doing?" she asks without greeting him. She pauses for a moment then says, "Okay, I'm switching it off." Layla turns off the TV, then asks, "Why can't we wat –" She pauses then puts the phone on speaker.

"Falcon says we can't watch the next piece," Layla explains.

"Hey, Kingsley," Falcon's voice comes over the phone. "Mason will kill me if you watched the next couple of minutes."

"Why? What's happening?" I ask, worried Mason will get into trouble.

"Give us forty minutes, and we'll be back, then Mason will explain everything to you."

"Okay."

I begin chewing on my bottom lip, just hoping the guys get home safely. I didn't expect anything like this to happen.

"Let's watch Grace and Frankie until they get back," Layla says.

"And stuff our faces," I add as I reach for the candy.

We're almost done watching a second episode when there's a knock at the door. I dart up, sending the popcorn flying over the table and floor. But when I open and see it's Falcon, I mutter, "Layla, it's your man."

Falcon grins at Layla while I get down on my knees so I can clean up the mess I've made.

Worry begins to grow at a rapid pace inside of me. "Isn't Mason back yet?" I ask, keeping my head down.

"He is. He went to change out of the suit," Falcon explains, making the anxiety ease in my chest.

Lifting my head, I smile. "Thanks."

When they begin to leave, I set the bowl aside and get up. "Enjoy the evening, guys."

"Catch you later," Layla throws over her shoulder while they walk toward the elevator.

I lean back against the door jamb as I watch them whisper to each other, and when the elevator doors close behind them, I sit down on the floor.

I'm being stupid now, waiting for him like this.

I pull my legs up and hug them to my chest, resting my chin on my knees. The numbers on the elevator begin to count down, and I hold my breath... until it passes by my floor.

Ugh... I hate waiting.

Why did he have to go change first?

The numbers start to count their way up, and when it ends on Mason's floor, a smile slowly stretches over my face.

It comes down to my floor, and the second the doors begin to open, my heart starts to race, but seeing Preston makes me feel like a deflated balloon.

"Oh, hey," Preston greets as he walks to his door. "Why are you sitting in the doorway?"

"I wanted some fresh air," I lie.

Preston glances around as if he can see the damn air, then states, "Why don't you go outside then? You're breathing in stale AC air."

Dude, you're way too practical.

"Thanks," I mumble, as I get up and pull my door shut. Letting out a sigh, I walk to the elevator.

"Enjoy," he calls out as I step into the stupid elevator.

"Why the hell am I even going outside? I could've gone out on the balcony," I snap at myself. "Kingsley, this is so not you. Get your shit together!" I press the button to take me back to my floor, and I'm glad to see Preston has gone into his suite.

When I reach my own door, and I pat my pockets for my keycard, I close my eyes and bang my head against the door.

"Ugh… Hunt! You're an idiot!" My shoulders slump as I drag my feet back to the freaking elevator, but glaring at it, I grumble, "This is all your fault." I take the stairs down and head out of the building to the main office so they can come unlock my door for me.

Mason

The fucking suit feels like it's suffocating me. I don't know how I'm going to get used to wearing one every day once I start working.

Preston will keep an eye on the internet to make sure the footage doesn't pop up anywhere, just in case someone managed to download it while it was airing.

I have no idea how Preston is able to do any of the shit he does, but he's brilliant. After today there's no way I'm letting go of him. He will be a huge asset to our new business.

It's actually scary how quick he can set something up online, and then make it disappear the next.

My phone vibrates, and when I open the email notification, the corner of my mouth lifts. It's an email from an unknown sender, and opening it, I see the Anonymous calling card along with the footage we aired today. It's the proof I'll need for the court case against the Senator and Serena.

This way, it won't create any suspicions that I was involved, and only Preston and I have the video.

I finish changing into a pair of jeans and a sweater.

Now that my revenge is almost complete, worry begins to creep into my mind. What if Kingsley doesn't understand?

"Start by telling her the video isn't out there. Get the important shit across so she doesn't have time to get angry," I advise myself as I walk out of the bedroom.

"Yeah, otherwise your ass is grass, and she's the lawnmower," Lake mumbles from the couch.

Placing a hand over my heart, I shoot him a glare, "Wow, thanks for the encouragement, buddy."

"Always a pleasure, babe," he quotes my saying while wagging his eyebrows.

"Later," I chuckle before I shut the door behind me.

When I get to Kingsley's suite, and there's no answer, I frown. I pull my phone out and bring up her number, but after a couple of rings, it goes to voicemail.

Fuck.

Did she find out already?

Falcon said they didn't watch.

I pull up Falcon's number as I take the stairs down to the lobby, so the call doesn't cut in the elevator.

"I love you, buddy, but your timing sucks," he grumbles when he answers.

"Layla and Kingsley didn't watch the footage, right?"

"No, they switched off the TV."

"Did you see Kingsley since you got back?"

"Yeah, I got Layla from Kingsley's suite," he mentions. "What's going on?"

"She's not answering her door or phone. For a minute, I thought she found out about us airing her near-drowning on television before I got to explain things to her."

"Did Kingsley say she was going somewhere?" he asks Layla.

"No, she was waiting for Mason," Layla answers. "Wait, maybe she went to get some coffee?"

"Did you hear that?" Falcon asks.

"Yeah, thanks. I'll check around campus for her."

I shove the phone into my pocket and walking out of the building, I head in the direction of the café on campus.

"Dude, I saw you on TV," a student says with excitement as I walk by him.

"Mason," a girl calls out, and I cringe inwardly as I keep walking. "You looked so hot."

"Mr. President!" I hear Kingsley's voice, and I stop so fast someone bumps into my back. I don't bother listening to the idiot's apology as my eyes scan over the campus. When I catch sight of her practically bouncing up and down as she jogs toward me, a smile spreads over my face.

Noticing she's not slowing down, I turn to face her direction, and as she gets to me, she jumps. I grab hold of her and chuckle when a high-pitched squeal leaves her while she practically wraps herself around me.

Holding onto my shoulders, Kingsley pulls slightly back, and her face is alight with a look of pride and excitement. She presses a hard kiss to my mouth, then begins to bounce in my arms.

"You can be lucky you're a short shit," I chuckle at her.

"Why?"

"Otherwise, you'd be eating grass with the way you're bouncing in my arms."

She grins, "I'm just so proud of you, hot stuff."

"Hot stuff?" I grumble.

She wags her eyebrows. "You can be glad I wasn't there. I would've jumped your bones on national television."

I turn and begin to walk back to the dorm with her still clinging to me like a monkey. "Are you into making pornos, Hunt?"

Her eyelashes lower over her eyes, and she licks her lips. Wrapping her arms around my neck, she brings her mouth to my ear and bites it softly before she whispers, "As long as it's your cock inside of me, I don't care where we are."

Fuck my life.

I'm going to shoot my load if she does that again.

Entering the lobby, I rush over to the elevator at record speed. When we step inside, she pulls back a little and tries to look all innocent as she says, "I'm locked out of my suite. They're printing me a new card."

I let go of her ass. "Legs down."

She listens, and when she's standing, she widens her eyes, "Oooh... in here?"

"You have a kinky side, I *really* want to know more about." My voice rumbles low because she is turning me on like never before in my life.

I press the number for my floor and lower my head so our faces are inches apart. "As badly as I want to hear you scream, you're going to have to be quiet because everyone's in my suite."

"I can't make any promises," she says, and reaching for my sweater, she pushes her hands underneath and lets them glide over my abs.

The doors ping open, and I pull one of her hands out from under my sweater and hold it as I stalk out of the elevator.

Chapter 27

Kingsley

When we walk into the suite, Lake says, "That was quick." Then he lifts his head and seeing us, a grin spreads over his face. "Okaayyy... I'm going to go eat something somewhere."

Grabbing his keys, he wags his eyebrows at us before he leaves. "Practice safe sex, kids. I'm too young to become a grandfather."

Mason lets out a chuckle as he pulls me toward his room, and the moment we step inside, he shuts and locks the door.

Placing an arm around me, he moves closer to me. "We have to talk first."

I pout, not liking the idea of that. "Can't we talk and get it on at the same time?"

A hot as hell smirk pulls at his lips, and he leans down, "You want me to fuck you, Hunt?"

I begin to nod as fast as I can without spraining something and ramble. "Badly. Like, you have no idea how badly. Seeing you in that suit –"

My words are cut short as Mason's mouth crashes against mine. His tongue dives into my mouth, and not wasting time, I kiss him back.

I step out of my shoes, right before he breaks the kiss and pushes me back onto the bed. I watch him with a huge smile as he almost rips my sweatpants and panties off. But when he unzips his jeans, the smile fades, and I can't help but lick my lips.

"Get your shirt off," he snaps as he yanks his sweater off.

I pull the fabric over my head and let out a shriek of laughter when he grabs hold of my thighs and yanks me toward the edge of the bed.

When he slams his cock into me, my back arches off the bed, and I grab hold of the covers.

Holy crap, I can't get enough of this man. My non-existent sex drive from before he came along is quickly getting out of control.

He braces himself over me with his left hand, pressing on the bed, and brings his right hand to my hip.

"You wanted to talk," I tease as he pulls back until only the head of his cock is still inside me.

"We can talk during the intermission," he grumbles as he fills me again with a hard thrust.

Breathless, I ask, "Intermission?"

"I plan to keep you naked all night." He drives into me so hard it shifts my body upward and makes a moan of pleasure burst over my parted lips.

I'm in seventh heaven when his strokes become harder, each one hitting deep within me. When my orgasm crashes over me, tightening every muscle in my body, I bow off the bed. Another moan escapes, and with the pleasure growing inside of me, it soon has me crying out.

Mason covers my mouth with his hand, muffling my sounds of ecstasy. My eyes lock on his as he unravels my mind and body with wave after wave of pure bliss, and seeing the rapture tightening his features as he empties himself inside of me, makes the moment perfect.

He slumps over me, catching himself just in time from landing on me.

"Fuck," he whispers breathlessly.

Now that he's closer, I bring my hands up to his arms and rub up and down them.

I smile into his eyes as I say, "Thanks, hot stuff."

"Why hot stuff?" He pulls out, and pleasure ripples over his body again.

"I'm testing pet names for you to see which one I like best," I explain.

He sits down and falls back onto the mattress, looking totally sated.

When I scoot off the bed, he says, "I liked hearing you scream Mr. President from the other side of the campus."

"One second." I clench my legs together and not caring what I look like, I do the freaking penguin walk to the bathroom.

When I'm done, and I walk back into his room, he pats the bed. "Get your sexy ass over here."

Grinning, I lie down next to him. He throws the covers over me as well, then he lifts his arm, so I can snuggle up against his side.

"So, Mr. President, let's talk."

"First thing. Only call me that when I can fuck you."

I let out a burst of laughter. "Noted, sir."

"That as well," he adds. "Sir and Mr. President are for the bedroom."

"And hot stuff?" I ask, pouting up at him.

He lifts an eyebrow at me. "How about just calling me Mason?"

"Let's negotiate," I say. "Can I call you Mace?"

"Mace works," he agrees, then he asks, "While we're talking about pet names, is there a story behind your father calling you Tiger?"

"It was kitten until I started PMSing," I explain.

Mason tries to keep from laughing, but when I snort, he cracks up. "You must've traumatized your father for him to switch from Kitten to Tiger."

I watch him laugh, and it fills me with so much happiness.

His laughter dies down, and our eyes meet. We turn on our sides and laying face to face we stare at each other for a while, and it fills my chest with something I haven't felt before.

It's fresh and light, making me feel safe and secure.

I like you, Mace.

He brings a hand to my face and brushes his fingers along my temple.

"Can I tell you something I haven't told anyone?" he whispers.

I nod.

"You scare me, Hunt." A frown begins to form on my face, but then he continues, "I've fallen for you."

273

"Why does that scare you?" I ask, keeping my voice soft so I don't disturb the moment between us.

"I almost lost you." He pauses and wrapping an arm around my waist, he holds me close.

I place my arm around him and begin to draw lazy patterns on his back.

"There was a moment I thought you were dead." He lets out a hollow-sounding chuckle. "I remember thinking you're too young to die. You have too much life in you to... just die."

He's quiet for a minute, and I keep moving my hand over his back. I never thought my dying, or almost dying, would have such an impact on the people around me. It's a sobering thought, realizing you make a difference in someone's life. Enough for them to mourn you.

"It felt like I lost something important, like you were just torn from my heart. That's when I realized how much you meant to me."

"I'm sorry it happened that way," I whisper, wishing it could have been different.

"Honestly, I wouldn't have admitted it otherwise. Nearly losing you showed me how much I've distanced myself from everyone but Falcon and Lake."

He presses a kiss to the tip of my nose before pulling back to meet my eyes. "You were literally a light that forced your way through the darkness I became accustomed to after I lost my sister."

I smile and press a kiss to his chin. "I like that. I can be your light while you're my heart." I shoot up and begin to bounce on the bed. "I'm hungry. Can we grab some food after we're done talking?"

"You and Lake aren't related, right?" he jokes as he pushes himself into a sitting position, leaning back against the headboard.

"He's my brother from another mother."

Mason's gaze slowly sweeps over my naked body. When he meets my eyes again, a grin pulls at his mouth. "I love how comfortable you are in your own skin."

Shrugging, I say, "I might not have the biggest ta-tas, or the best curves, but I like the way I look."

"I like the way you look as well," he teases and bringing a hand to my chest, he brushes his knuckles over my nipple.

"Was that all you wanted to talk about?" I ask.

Mason shakes his head, and a serious look settles on his face. "You watched some of what happened today, right?"

Immediately a smile splits across my face. "Yeah, and you looked badass up on the stage."

He winks at me, and it's a good thing I'm not wearing any panties, or they would've melted right off.

He brushes my hair back over my shoulder, then says, "Hear me out before you respond, okay."

"Okay."

"Preston is good with computers."

Huh?

He smiles when he sees my confusion, then continues, "I needed you to know that because he compiled the footage we aired today. As soon as it was done airing, he deleted it from the internet, so it's not out there."

"Okay."

"You saw with Layla's incident we blurred all the faces out except for Serena's?" Mason asks, and I begin to get a niggling suspicion where this is going.

"Yes, I'm glad you did that."

"We did the same thing with the footage we got from the indoor pool."

With a hawk eye, he watches for my reaction.

"But Preston took it down, so it's not out there, right?" I ask to make sure I understood him.

"Yes, only Preston and I have a copy, so I have the evidence to hand over to the DA's office, for them to proceed with prosecuting the Senator and Serena."

"Prosecute?" I ask.

"Yes, so the Senator can be charged with embezzlement and Serena with assault."

There's a twinge of sadness for Serena, but it vanishes as quickly as it comes. "Am I a horrible person for feeling…" my words trail away when I realize I'm not sure how I feel, "relieved?"

Emotion floods me like a tidal wave when I realize the full impact of what has happened today. When tears rush to my eyes, I look down at my hands where they're resting on my leg. A tear splats against my knee, and I quickly swipe it away.

"Babe?" Mason shifts closer to me, and placing a finger under my chin, he nudges my face up. "Are you okay?"

Meeting his eyes, I whisper, "You kept your promise."

"I told you I would," he replies with his worried eyes not leaving mine.

"You did all of that for me?"

He nods, and the corner of his mouth curves up. "Don't you know I'll do anything for you?"

The moment makes me finally comprehend the relationship between Mason and me is really happening. We're not just fooling around.

"Thank you, Mace." I shuffle closer to him on my knees and framing his face with my hands, I say, "Thank you for not letting me die." I struggle to stay in control of my emotions as tears spill over my cheeks. "Thank you for making her pay."

Through my tears, my eyes caress every inch of Mason's face, and I feel a fluttering in my chest. It's deep and warm, and it fills me with hope and dreams. It's knowing, Mason won't hurt me, and it's safe to dream of a future with him.

I lean forward and press a soft kiss to his lips, then I whisper, "I just fell for you."

Chapter 28

Mason

I finish up my work and checking my watch, I see that it's almost time for dinner. I close the laptop and head to the living room where Lake's in his usual spot.

"Have you ordered food?" I ask as I sit down on the other couch.

"Is that a trick question?" he quips.

"Just checking."

"Falcon ran down to get the Chinese. He'll also call the girls and Preston on his way back up." Lake doesn't take his eyes away from his phone.

"Are you texting with Lee-ann?" I ask. "She's arriving this Saturday, right?"

"Yes, Lee's flight is landing at three pm." He smiles as he sets his phone down.

"You already shortened her name?" I ask.

"We're getting married in July," he answers wryly.

"Right, I guess it's not too soon," I agree. Even though I've asked him a million times by now, I can't stop from asking again, "Are you sure about this marriage?"

He takes a deep breath and lets it out slowly. "Not a hundred percent."

His answer shocks me. "Why?"

"I'll only know for sure once we've spent some time together. For me to say I have no doubts at this stage would be stupid."

"True."

Falcon opens the door and comes in carrying bags with Chinese take out. The girls and Preston follow right behind him.

When Kingsley moves to sit down next to me, I take hold of her hips and pull her down on my lap.

She immediately smiles and presses a kiss to my cheek. "I haven't seen you in forever," she jokes.

"Right," I grin back at her. "It's been like... four hours." I let out a chuckle, and my eyes land on Lake, who's watching us with a warm smile.

He tilts his head, and a rare serious expression settles on his face. "You have no idea how happy it makes me seeing the two of you together."

"Thanks, buddy," I reply, knowing he means every word.

Layla sets the food out on the dinner table, then calls, "Get your butts over here so we can eat."

Lake's up like a flash, which has me chuckling. I help Kingsley up and walk over to the table. Pulling out a chair for her, I wait until she's seated before I take the one next to her.

The conversation is light while we eat, and I wait until everyone is done before I take Serena's phone from my pocket and set it down on the table.

"The reason I wanted us all to meet for dinner is that Serena told me something right before the stadium erupted in chaos."

"What?" Kingsley asks, leaning her elbows on the table.

I turn on the phone and bring up the messages between Serena and Mrs. Reyes.

My eyes go to Falcon, and I hand him the phone.

He reads the texts, and then his mouth sets in a hard line.

"How do you want to handle this?" I ask him, feeling it's only right he makes the decision, seeing as it involves his mother.

He sets the phone down on the table, then bites the words out, "The same way we handled Serena. We destroy her." He pinches the bridge of his nose and takes a couple of deep breaths before he looks at Layla. He reaches for her hand and holding it he explains to everyone else what's going on, "Serena told Clare that she saw you had an allergy when she looked at your student file. Clare was the one who told her what to do."

There's a couple of seconds of silence before Lake asks, "Preston, can you hack into the bank and freeze her credit cards?"

"I haven't done it before, but I can try," Preston answers, already looking excited.

Falcon lets out a bitter chuckle and shakes his head. "That's not good enough. I want to hit her where it will hurt most."

"Her status," I murmur.

"I'll have to talk to Julian and my father about this."

"You want to go into the office tomorrow and see them?" I ask.

"We could always join our fathers for a round of golf. Mine keeps asking," Lake mentions.

"That's a good idea," Falcon agrees. "Do you know on which days they like to play?"

"Thursday afternoons," Lake answers.

"Tomorrow." Falcon begins to nod. "I'll call Julian and tell him to meet us at the golf club."

"So, you don't need me to hack into anything?" Preston asks, looking a little disappointed.

"Sorry, buddy," Lake pats his shoulder, and it makes Falcon's lips twitch. "Maybe next time."

"Are you okay?" I ask Falcon. Even though he doesn't get along with Clare, she's still his mother at the end of the day.

There's a cynical pull on his face, "Can't say I'm surprised by any of this." He pauses and lets out a sigh, "I'm okay, though."

His eyes meet Layla's, and he whispers, "I'm sorry, my rainbow."

She looks at him with so much love, it makes my heart feel at ease, knowing she won't blame him for his mother's actions. "Don't apologize to me, Falcon. None of it was your doing."

"Well, it's a relief knowing I didn't almost kill my best friend," Kingsley suddenly mumbles.

"You know I never blamed you," Layla says.

"I know, but it didn't take the guilt away." Kingsley shakes her head. "Why do people have to be so mean? Why can't everyone just get along?"

"Greed," Preston answers her. "The more you have, the more you want, and the more ruthless you become to get it." His eyes widen when he realizes what he just said, and then he sputters, "I-I don't m-m-mean you guys."

"No, you're right," Lake agrees wryly. "That's why I won't join CRC." His eyes lock on mine. "I'm not strong enough to not let that kind of power change me."

"It's an intense feeling," I admit. "You're instantly on a high."

"I wish I was twenty-one," Kingsley says. "I'd love a drink right now."

I begin to laugh and shake my head at her. "When's your birthday? I'll make sure there's plenty to drink for your twenty-first."

"It's on the nineteenth of July. I'm cancer."

"I don't know shit about star signs," I mutter.

"When's your birthday?" she asks.

"February fifth," I answer.

"That explains everything," Layla says, and she begins to chuckle.

"What?" I ask.

"You're Aquarius, dude."

"So?"

"Aquarius are detached, stubborn, and no middle path exists for them," Preston reads off his phone.

Pointing at Preston, Layla tries to hold back her laughter. "What he said."

"Your birthday is around the corner," Lake murmurs. "We need to organize something."

"Let's get through the next week. Turning twenty-three is nothing in the grand scheme of things," I say, just wanting all this shit to be in the past already.

"I hate wearing caps," I grumble when Lake holds one out to me.

"You're going to burn out in the sun. Take the damn thing," he orders.

I take it and pull it onto my head. "Are we early?"

"Here they come," Falcon says.

I turn my head in the direction he's looking, and then a smile breaks out over my face. Mr. Reyes walks in front with Mr. Cutler right behind him and my father's at the back.

"Preston asked me why we don't walk next to each other." I point at our fathers. "I should just take a photo and send it to him."

Falcon chuckles. "I never noticed it until you pointed it out."

"At least we inherited all the good traits," Lake quips.

"Boys," Mr. Reyes greets when he reaches us. "I'm glad you finally decided to join us. Julian just called. He's waiting by the golf carts for us. "

Falcon walks with Mr. Reyes, and I grin when Lake throws his arm around Mr. Cutler's shoulders.

Dad smiles at me, then he tilts his head. "You look different."

"It's the stupid cap," I grumble.

"If you say so." The corner of his mouth pulls up. "Have you met anyone interesting lately?" he asks while we follow behind the others.

"Like who?"

"Oh… anyone," his grin grows into a smile, "like a girl?"

"Who told you?" I ask, letting out a chuckle.

"Your mom went for her usual botox and got to talking with the good doctor."

"Noooo. Dr. Hunt?" I stop and cover my mouth with a hand. "I'm too scared to ask what they talked about."

Dad pats me on the shoulder. "Your mother was gushing all night long about how the doctor sang your praises. So, tell me, are you serious about the girl?"

As we near the golf carts, I meet my father's eyes and nod. "Very."

"As long as you're happy, Mace."

Emotion wells in my chest. "I am, Dad. I really am."

"You should bring her for dinner. Your mother would love to meet her."

I nod and then turn my head to Julian as he finishes greeting Lake and Mr. Cutler.

"Mr. Chargill." Julian and Dad shake hands, and then he waits for Dad to join the others before he holds his hand out to me.

Shaking hands, I'm already feeling emotional after my talk with Dad, and it has me swallowing before I say, "Thank you."

"For what?" Julian asks, a look of confusion washing over his face.

"For trusting me."

A wide smile stretches over his face. "I'll always have your back, Mason."

"For a while, I forgot that," I admit.

Julian nods, and the sadness in his eyes tells me his thoughts immediately went to Jennifer.

My breathing speeds up, and I have to look away when the emotion pushes up my throat. I focus on a tree to the side of Julian, and say, "She would want you to be happy."

"Look at me, Mace."

I shake my head, not trusting my voice.

Julian places his hands on my shoulders, then repeats, "Look at me."

I take a deep breath and bring my eyes back to his face.

"Jennifer was my first love. No matter where this life will take me, she will always be in my heart. One day I might meet a woman who I can see myself settling down with, but that will not mean I've forgotten Jen. You know that, right?"

"I do, and for what it's worth, I hope you find someone who can make you happy."

Julian moves an arm around my shoulder, and we slowly walk toward our family.

"It means a lot to me to hear you say that." He lets out a breath. "Now, let's kick some ass."

"You're holding it wrong," Mr. Cutler tells Lake for what feels like the hundredth time.

"Dad, I'm left-handed," Lake reminds him.

"Oh, right."

"Well, don't I feel loved right now," Lake jokes as he whacks the ball.

Falcon lets out a burst of laughter when a piece of grass flies into the air, and the ball only rolls a couple of inches.

I pretend to cough as I say, "Missed."

Lake pulls a face at me before he tries again.

Another piece of grass shoots into the air. "If you carry on like that, I'm going to have to replace the entire green by the time you're done," Mr. Cutler mutters.

"Thanks, Dad," Lake says wryly.

Falcon laughs again, and it has Lake pointing the club at him. "You come hit the damn ball."

"Dear Lord, I'm watching the blind lead the blind," Mr. Reyes gripes. "Let me just hit the ball so we can move on."

We all stand back, and as Mr. Reyes pulls his club back, Julian shouts, "Dad, duck!"

Mr. Reyes smacks the ball totally in the wrong direction, and then he looks up at the sky. "Where?"

"What do you mean, where?" Julian asks as he begins to laugh.

"You said there was a duck."

Lake sinks to his butt, silent laughter making tears trickle over his cheeks while he points a shaking finger at Mr. Reyes.

"Todd, your boy's going to wet himself," Mr. Reyes says while trying not to smile.

"Dad, I meant you had to duck down," Julian explains, and then he cracks up.

"Then tell me to take cover. Don't yell duck when we're right by a pond."

I cover my face with my hand as my body begins to shake.

Then Mr. Reyes asks, "Why did you yell duck, anyway?"

"For god's sake, Warren, he was distracting you," Dad calls out from behind me. "Sometimes, I wonder where your head's at."

"I can tell you where my club's going to be shortly," Mr. Reyes threatens as he sets after Julian, who can barely run from all the laughing.

"You're going to give yourself a heart attack," Mr. Cutler calls after Mr. Reyes.

Mr. Reyes stops and walking back to us, a smile forms on his face. My eyes dart to Falcon, where he's watching his father with a smile around his own mouth.

I wish I could freeze time as I glance at the men around me. Every one of us is smiling.

"Mason," Dad says as he walks by me. "You want to race?"

"Hell, yeah." I dart forward, not having to be asked twice.

"Oh God, we're all going to die," Mr. Cutler mumbles.

I climb into the cart that's closest to the green and smirk at my father as he gets into the other one.

Falcon takes the seat next to me, while Lake and Julian climb into the backseats.

I wait for Mr. Reyes and Mr. Cutler to get onto Dad's cart before I start the engine.

"You ready, Dad?" I call out.

Dad nods.

"If they beat us, I won't live it down at the office, so you better win," Julian says from behind me.

Mr. Reyes holds a club up in the air and begins the countdown, "Three... two... one..."

Dad pulls away, and I let him get ahead of me before I begin to drive.

"Are you losing on purpose?" Lake asks. "They won't give you a bonus for letting them win."

"Sit back and enjoy the show. You won't get to see this again," I say, and I begin to speed up as we get near the bend in the road.

"Slowpoke!" Mr. Cutler calls out.

Dad glances over his shoulder, and when he sees me gaining on him, he tries to go faster just as he hits the bend.

"Asher!" Mr. Reyes yells as the cart begins to swing to the right.

I bring mine to a stop, and we sit and watch as our fathers drive right into the pond. A duck flies out of the nearby bushes, and then Mr. Reyes, mumbles, "We should've gone hunting."

Lake falls out of the cart and rolls onto his back, hardly able to catch his breath as he cracks up. Falcon's practically crying next to me. Julian hits the seat, tears streaming down his face.

I chuckle until I see our fathers try and help each other out of the water, but they keep dragging each other down. I have to hold my head as laughter tears through me.

"Stop wetting yourselves and come help us," Dad shouts.

Lake begins to wheeze. "Stop... can't... breathe."

Falcon gets out to go help them, but he only makes it to the grass before he sinks to his knees.

I climb out and wipe my eyes as I walk to them. Standing on the edge, I hold a hand out to my dad. He grabs hold of me with both his hands, and then he yanks hard, making my ass fly forward until cold water rushes over me.

Laughter explodes from Julian, Falcon, and Lake as I sit up in the water.

When I look up to Dad, there's a huge smile on his face. "Nice and cool, isn't it?"

He holds his hand out for me, and when I'm back on my feet again, I don't think and throw my arms around Dad, hugging him.

"It's fu…" I quickly correct my language, "It's good to see you smile."

"You, too, my boy."

Chapter 29

Mason

After changing our clothes, we all meet up at the clubhouse for some drinks.

Falcon waits until everyone has a glass in their hands, then he says, "I need your help with a problem."

Mr. Reyes' head snaps up, a look of worry flashing over his face. "It must be serious because you've never asked for help before."

"It's an unpleasant situation." Falcon takes out Serena's phone and pulling up the texts he hands it over to his father.

As Mr. Reyes reads the messages, his face sets into hard lines. "They did this to Layla?" His voice is low and threatening.

"Yes, sir."

Mr. Reyes nods, and for a moment, he stares at the table, and then his voice rumbles, "Asher, cut Clare off."

"Why?" Dad asks. He leans over to Mr. Reyes and looks at the phone. "Dear Lord."

"Stephanie's daughter almost died because of them," Mr. Reyes murmurs. "Todd, draw up the papers tomorrow. I want Clare out of my life without a settlement."

"You're divorcing Mom?" Julian asks, and when Mr. Reyes' eyes snap to him, Julian quickly adds, "I'm not against it."

"Dad," Falcon says, to get his father's attention. When they're eyes meet, Falcon continues, "That's not enough. I want her ruined. I want her to lose her status."

Mr. Reyes nods and thinks for a while.

"We could send these messages to the newspapers. That would ruin her social standing," Lake mentions.

Mr. Reyes shakes his head. "I think we should let this go to court." He looks at Mr. Cutler and hands him Serena's phone. "Do you still have that contact at the DA's office?"

"Yes, I can give him a call."

"Show him the messages and ask him if it's enough to prosecute her."

Mr. Cutler reads the messages. "Would Miss Weinstock be willing to testify? With that, they would be able to prosecute."

"Serena would use her testimony against Clare to get a plea bargain," Lake mumbles.

I look at Lake, frowning, "Are you telling me one of them is going to walk free?"

"No, Serena will still receive a sentence if found guilty. But it could be reduced," Mr. Cutler explains.

"Reduced to what?" I ask, not liking the sound of this at all.

"For example, she could be sentenced to a couple of months of community work." When I open my mouth, Mr. Cutler holds up his hand. "It's only an example, Mason. We'll push for the harshest punishment."

"Let's all take some time to think about this," Mr. Reyes says. "We need to have all our ducks in a row before we start this war."

"Serena can't get off with a tap on the wrist." Closing my eyes, I rub them. "I promised Kingsley."

"The girl you're dating?" Dad asks.

Mr. Reyes leans forward, his face looking like a thunder cloud. "What are you saying, Mason?"

"The girl on the footage is Kingsley," Lake answers for me.

Dad stands up and walks away from the table, and Mr. Reyes slowly rises to his feet, growling, "Why wasn't I made aware of this?"

"We had it handled," Julian answers.

"You knew about this?" Mr. Reyes slams a fist on the table. "My God."

"Sit down, Warren," Mr. Cutler murmurs, pulling at Mr. Reyes' arm. "I'll pay the DA's office a visit tomorrow morning."

I get up and whisper, "Excuse me." Walking to where Dad is standing out on the patio, I stop next to him and stare out over the green.

"Why didn't you tell me?" he whispers, his voice sounding drained of all the laughter we shared today.

I take a deep breath and let it out slowly. "Kingsley was my first priority. I didn't even think to tell you. Sorry, Dad."

"Don't apologize," Dad whispers. "If I had been more involved in your life, I would've been aware of what was happening."

Dad turns to me and placing his hand on my shoulders, he says, "We're going to win this. I will do everything in my power to help you."

I didn't know how badly I needed to hear those words until they leave his mouth.

My breathing speeds up, and I try to suppress the emotions, but when Dad pulls me to his chest, the wall breaks.

He wraps his arms tightly around me. "I'm here, son."

It takes every bit of strength I have to not cry, and my voice is shaky and hoarse when I say, "Serena almost killed the woman I love. I need to see her suffer."

"And she will," Dad says as he pulls back. Our eyes meet, and when I see the promise on his face, it makes the load on my shoulders feel lighter.

Kingsley

After I finally submit my assignment, I close my laptop and let out a sigh of relief.

"At least, that's done and taken care of."

I get up and stretch my body when there's a knock at the door. I hardly have the door open when Mason pushes his way inside and lifts me off my feet.

Laughter bubbles over my lips as I hug him back.

"Are you done with the assignment?" he asks as he sets me back down.

"I finished seconds ago."

He presses a kiss to my lips, then says, "There's something I want to do with you."

"Oooh… that sounds promising."

He smiles for a moment, but his expression quickly turns serious. "I know it might be too soon, and I'll understand if you're not ready, but I really want to teach you how to swim."

I didn't expect him to say that, so it takes my mind a couple of seconds to catch up. "Tonight?"

"I want to do it as soon as possible, but you have to be ready. I don't want to push you. If you're afraid of water then we –"

"I'm not afraid of water," I interrupt him. "I'm afraid of deep water." I bite my bottom lip, already feeling anxiety tightening in my stomach. "Can I learn in the shallow end?"

"Definitely," he answers quickly. "We don't have to do it all at once. Maybe we can just get in the pool tonight. Once you feel comfortable with that, we can take the next step."

"I like the sound of that more," I admit, some of the anxiety easing back.

"Do you have a swimsuit?" he asks.

I let out a burst of laughter then shake my head.

"That's okay. I booked a room with a private pool at *Hotel Bel-Air*, in case you agreed. We'll have more privacy there, and I didn't want your first time back in the water to be where the incident happened."

This man. Who knew he could be so caring?

"Should I just wear shorts and a t-shirt?" I ask.

"You can wear anything to the hotel," he answers, then he smirks. "You can swim butt naked. You won't hear me complaining."

"Now that's what I call a good incentive," I tease.

Walking into the presidential suite, my eyes widen for what feels like the hundredth time tonight.

"First, the helicopter ride and now this?" I ask as I glance around at all the extravagant luxury. "Not that I'm ungrateful, but... this is... a lot." I struggle to find the right words to express how I feel.

Mason wraps his arms around me from behind, and his voice rumbles in my ear, "Just say thank you so we can get naked."

"Thank you," I whisper. I turn around in his arms and smile up at him. "Thank you for doing all of this for me."

"Anything for you."

He lets go of me and walking to a door he opens it. "Is it okay if we keep the lights off outside, or do you want them on?"

"Off is fine. Just don't leave me alone in the dark," I answer as I come up behind him. "This place is so beautiful. If you had warned me, I could've worn something other than jeans and a t-shirt."

Mason glances over his shoulder, then frowns. "What's wrong with what you're wearing?"

"Mace, I look like I crawled out of the laundry basket."

"Well, take the clothes off, then it won't be a problem," he teases.

"Okay." Taking hold of my shirt, I pull it over my head and drop it on the floor. Mason leans back against the door jamb and watches me undress. "Are you swimming in your clothes?" I ask when I'm naked as the day I was born.

His mouth curves at the corner, and when I brush past him, walking out onto the patio, he says, "Seeing your sexy ass, I think we should check out the bedroom first."

I glance over my shoulder and let out a chuckle. "I thought we could see what sex is like in a pool."

"Works for me," he comments and quickly begins to drag his clothes off.

I bring my eyes back to the water, and the anxiety starts to grow until I fist my hands at my sides.

You can do this, Kingsley.

Mason's with you.

You can do this.

Mason presses his body against mine from behind, then says, "Go as slow as you need to."

I turn around and look up at him. "Can't you just throw me over your shoulder and jump in. Like last time. If I go slow, I'll never get in."

His eyes search over my face. "I'm not jumping into that pool with you, Kingsley." He tilts his head and thinks, then he begins to smile. He takes hold of my hips and lifts me, "Legs around my waist."

A smile instantly stretches over my face while I do what he says.

"You ready?" he asks, not taking his eyes away from mine.

I take a deep breath, then say, "Yes."

When he begins to walk toward the pool, I glance over my shoulder.

"Eyes on me, Hunt."

My head snaps back, and I keep my eyes on his even though he's looking past me to see where we're going. When he takes a step down, I tighten my arms around his neck.

"What music do you like?" he suddenly asks.

"Anything, as long as it makes sense," I ramble the answer off when my stomach begins to churn.

"Do you have a favorite song?"

I shake my head.

"How old were you when you lost your virginity?" he asks.

"Sixteen." He takes another step down, which has the words exploding from me, "It was in the back seat of Daniel's car. It smelled like old gym socks."

Mason moves forward, and when I feel the water lap at my butt, I cry, "Wait!" I almost climb up him as if he's a tree, but settle for hiding my face in his neck. My breaths explode over my lips. "Wait."

303

He tightens his arms around me. "I've got you." He presses a kiss to my shoulder, then says, "I like to surf. Going out at sunrise when everything is quiet, it's one of the best feelings."

"I-I bet you're good at it," I say breathlessly from the anxiety clawing its way up my spine.

"Lake is the best between the three of us. It's like he was born to be a surfer. The way he rides a wave... it's something to see."

I relax enough to ease back until I can look at Mason again. His eyes lock on mine. "Do you have any idea how beautiful you are in the moonlight?"

I let out a burst of air, not able to laugh right now.

Mason presses his forehead to mine, then whispers, "Do you trust me?"

I don't hesitate to answer, "Yes."

"I'm going to move forward, but I'll stop once the water touches my arms. Are you okay with that?"

I take a couple of deep breaths before I nod. I keep my eyes locked on his, and when the water begins to slowly climb up my lower back, Mason says, "Thank you for giving me a chance."

I nod, and emotion mixes with the anxiety making tears rush to my eyes.

"Thank you for never backing down when I gave you shit."

The water reaches my waist, and a wave of intense panic makes it hard to breathe.

Mason takes a deep breath, and I feel his chest press against mine. When he lets it out, his voice is incredibly calm as he says, "Breathe in with me."

When I feel his chest expand again, I suck in a desperate breath of air. I keep doing it until my breathing's back to normal.

A look of pride softens his features. "You did it, Kingsley."

"I did?"

He nods, then turns us around and wades his way back to the edge. He sits me down on the side and reaching for my face, he frames it with his hands.

"I'm so fucking proud of you."

I take hold of his forearms and smile against his mouth as he kisses me.

Chapter 30

Mason

Walking out of the building, I head in the direction of the café to find Kingsley after she texted that she was grabbing some hot chocolate.

We got back early this morning, and with all the excitement of getting her back in the water, I forgot to ask her whether she'll come to the airport with us to welcome Lee-ann and her family.

Glancing to my left, I see West come out of his dorm, and when his eyes land on me, I let out a heavy breath.

I have to stop this shit between us. We can't go on like this forever.

"Mason," he calls out as he jogs across the road. "I haven't seen you in a while. Have you been pulling weeds at Jennifer's grave?"

My first reaction is to let the rage take over, but I look back to the café, and when I see Kingsley walking toward me, I push the destructive emotions down.

You have to put an end to it now, Mason.

The last time you got into a fight with West, Kingsley got hurt.

"Did you hear me?" West asks as he comes up behind me, but I ignore him, keeping my eyes locked on the light of my life.

I'm on the cusp of starting a new life.

There's no place for anger and bitterness.

"Mason!" West shouts when I still don't respond to him.

Kingsley reaches me and taking hold of my hand, she links our fingers, her grip tight.

"Don't worry," I reassure her when I see the concern in her eyes. "He's not worth the time."

"Oh, that's rich," West chuckles, coming to a standstill right by us.

Kingsley looks at West. "You have to stop this."

He smirks at her, happy about the reaction he's getting from her.

I lock eyes with West. "It's sad, Dayton. What we've been doing for the past five years, is just so unbelievably sad. I'm done living my life like this. Go see a therapist and deal with your shit. Stop baiting me, hoping I'll beat you up so it will ease your guilt."

"I wasn't aware you majored in Psych 101," he sneers, but I don't miss the flash of agony and guilt in his eyes. "I don't feel guilty," he spits out. "She was the one spinning everywhere over the fucking road and causing chaos. Everyone on that road was lucky, she was the only one who died."

Kingsley steps closer to me, and just knowing she's by my side helps me to keep the deep-rooted rage from exploding like an erupting volcano.

I take a breath, and knowing it's time to start honoring my sister, instead of tainting her memory with guilt and anger, I say, "I'm going to let my sister rest in peace."

West lets out an anxious chuckle when he sees that baiting me isn't getting his desired result any longer. "So, you're going to give up? Is that what you're saying." He takes a step closer to me, which has Kingsley reacting and moving in front of me. His eyes drop to her. "Are you his bodyguard now?"

Before Kingsley can answer, I say, "I'm done with you, Dayton. You're nothing but empty noise."

Pulling at Kingsley's hand, I begin to walk back to our building.

"You're really going to let me get away with murdering Jennifer? Some fucking brother, you are," he shouts after me.

"Let me have a sip of that," I say to Kingsley doing my best to ignore West.

She quickly hands me the beverage, and I take a gulp of the warm liquid before I hand it back to her, then I pull a face. "Damn, Hunt. Did you add extra sugar in there?"

"Only five." She grins. "What? Did you think I was just a naturally sweet person?"

"There's nothing sweet about you," I grumble.

"Mason!" West yells. "Don't fucking walk away from me!"

As we enter our dorm, Kingsley looks up at me with pride shining from her eyes. "Are you okay?"

I nod and press the button for the elevator. "I still want to kill him, but I meant everything I said. The accident wasn't anyone's fault, and West needs to move on. It's time to leave the past where it belongs instead of dragging it along with me. He has to deal with his own guilt."

"It must've been hard hearing him say all those things." Kingsley brings our joint hands to her mouth and presses a kiss to the back of mine. "But I'm really proud of how you handled it."

We step into the elevator, and I lean down, pressing a kiss to Kingsley's mouth. "I'm sorry you got hurt because of me last time we had a fight."

"Hey, I got you to give me first aid. Not every girl can say that," she teases.

"Hunt, you're the only girl who can say that."

When we get to Van Nuys Airport, I park behind Lake. Turning off the engine, I look to where Dad is standing with Mr. Reyes, Mr. Cutler, and Julian.

"Are you sure it's okay for me to be here?" Kingsley asks, and she begins to chew at her bottom lip.

I reach over and free her lip from between her teeth. "I'm sure. Come, let me formally introduce you to my father."

I get out and walk around the back of the car, and opening the door for Kingsley, I reach my hand out to her.

She takes hold of me and climbing out, her eyes instantly dart in my father's direction.

I link our fingers and shut the door, then begin to head toward the group.

"He already likes you, so you have nothing to worry about," I murmur as we get close.

"Excuse me, Warren," Dad says when he sees us. A smile forms on his face, and he takes a couple of steps in our direction. "This must be Kingsley." Dad offers his hand to her, his eyes quickly sweeping over her.

Kingsley shakes his hand. "It's a pleasure meeting you, sir."

"The pleasure is all mine." Dad keeps smiling at her, then he says, "Dynamite comes in small packages. Looking at you, the saying must be true."

"Thank you, sir." Kingsley's neck flushes red, and it has me grinning.

Looking at Dad, I ask, "Are you ready?"

"Yes, Park Je-ha is no easy man to deal with, but I believe we're ready."

"We'll wait over by the cars until they land," Falcon says after he and Layla greeted Julian and Mr. Reyes.

"We'll join you." Patting Dad's shoulder, I say, "Good luck."

"Thanks, son." He turns back to the others but then stops. "You should bring Kingsley for dinner."

"Next Sunday?" I ask.

"Perfect."

When we get back to the cars, I lean against my Bugatti. Turning Kingsley around, so she's facing the landing strip, I pull her back so she can lean against me. I wrap my arms around her and rest my chin on top of her head.

After a couple of minutes, she asks, "Are you nervous about meeting her?"

"Not as nervous as Lake," I murmur and glancing to where Lake is standing next to his father, I can't keep the worry for my friend from growing in my heart.

"Does CRC really need this deal?" Kingsley asks.

Earlier I explained to her that Mr. Park will be investing a substantial amount, which will help CRC reach a whole new level on the global front.

"If we want to expand, then yes, we do."

"I hope she's good to Lake," she whispers.

"She better be," I grumble.

The private jet begins its descent, and when it touches down, Lake walks to where we are all waiting.

"I look okay, right?" he asks.

"Lake, she's so lucky to have you," Layla says. "You look as handsome as ever."

"You've got this, buddy. We're right behind you," Falcon encourages him.

"One look at you, and she'll be swept off her feet," Kingsley adds.

When Lake looks at me, I point to my car. "It's not too late to leave."

"Thanks, Mace," he grumbles, then he grins at me, probably thinking I was joking. "Did you hear that noise on the way here?" he asks.

Lake came in my car, so I could drive his Koenigsegg Regera. The past two days he's been complaining about hearing a whistling sound every time he speeds up.

"I didn't hear shit, but I'll drive her back to the Academy to make sure."

"I'll leave it be if you don't hear the sound by the time we get back." He walks over to Julian, who is waiting with our fathers.

Letting go of Kingsley, I stand up straight and adjust my suit jacket.

"It's showtime," I whisper.

"Good luck." Kingsley presses a kiss to my cheek and waits with Layla, while Falcon and I go to join the rest of the group where they're standing.

Minutes later, two guards exit the plane first, followed by people who look like the administrative staff.

When another man begins to descend the stairs, Lake and Mr. Reyes begin to move forward. My eyes glue themselves to the exit door of the plane as I wait for Lee-ann to appear.

A middle-aged woman exits after the man and only then does Lee-ann follow. Her face is expressionless as she pauses in the opening, her eyes on the back of her father.

Her poise is unyielding as she climbs down the stairs, and she ignores the hand a guard offers to help her down the last couple of steps.

She stops a couple of feet behind her father, her eyes downcast.

"She's like ice," I whisper to Falcon.

"Maybe she's nervous."

Mr. Reyes shakes hands with Mr. Park, and says, "It's an honor having you visit us again, Chairman Park. Welcome."

When one of the administrative staff begins to translate the greeting, my eyes widen. "They can't speak English?"

"How did the two of you communicate," Falcon asks.

"Lee's fluent," Lake grumbles. "Now, shut up and smile."

After all the men are done being introduced, Mr. Park says something in Korean, which has Lee-ann moving forward.

She stops a couple of feet in front of Lake and folding her hands over her stomach, she bows, her posture still stiff as fuck.

"Good afternoon," her eyes meet Lake's for the first time, "I will do my best as your future wife, Mr. Cutler."

Holy fuck.

There's so much wrong with this picture I don't even know where to begin to make sense of it.

Driving back to the Academy, I'm stuck in my head as I replay the afternoon's events, while my eyes are on my car in front of me, which Lake is driving.

He didn't even get a moment alone with Lee-ann. She stuck to her father's side like glue.

"Are you worried?" Kingsley asks.

"I am. That's not what I expected," I admit.

"Lake seems okay with how things went," she mentions.

"That's his specialty. The more he worries, the more he smiles and jokes."

A couple of miles from the campus, my phone rings. Seeing Lake's name, I put it on speaker, "What's up?"

"I'm hungry. I'm going to stop for pizza. You want me to bring you some?"

"Anything with pineapple on it," Kingsley says, which has me shuddering because fruit does not belong on pizza.

"And you, Mace?" he asks.

"Anything that doesn't have fruit on it," I joke, shooting Kingsley a grin. "Oh, and by the way, I still don't hear the sound. Are you sure your windows weren't open when you heard it?"

"Yeah, that's probably it. Thanks for checking it out."

The call ends, and at the next intersection, Lake turns left. I glance at the back of my Bugatti before I speed up to close the gap left between Falcon and me.

OJAI, California – Vehicle accident kills one and hospitalizes one other.

The community of Ojai, which has long been known as a haven for artists, has been brutally shaken by the traumatic events which took place outside the prestigious Trinity Academy.

Ojai is a vibrant place with unique, natural beauty, nestled in the mountains just 12 miles inland from the Pacific Ocean and is the smallest city in Ventura County.

Emergency services responded to a vehicle accident outside the gates of the college late this afternoon.

A student of the Academy was killed on impact. The state of the other student is still unknown.

To be continued in <u>Lake</u>'s book.

Trinity Academy

Enemies To Lovers

Heartless

Novel #1

Carter Hayes & Della Truman

Reckless

Novel #2

Logan West & Mia Daniels

Careless

Novel #3

Jaxson West & Leigh Baxter

Ruthless

Novel #4

Marcus Reed & Willow Brooks

Shameless

Novel #5

Rhett Daniels & Evie Cole

Connect with me

Newsletter

FaceBook

Amazon

GoodReads

BookBub

Instagram

Twitter

Website

About the author

Michelle Heard is a Bestselling Romance Author who loves creating stories her readers can get lost in. She loves an alpha hero who is not afraid to fight for his woman.

Want to be up to date with what's happening in Michelle's world? Sign up to receive the latest news on her alpha hero releases → NEWSLETTER

If you enjoyed this book or any book, please consider leaving a review. It's appreciated by authors.

Acknowledgments

Sheldon, you're my rainbow. Thank you for all the color you add to my life.

To my beta readers, Kelly, Elaine, Sarah, and Sherrie - Thank you for being the godparents of my paper-baby.

Sheena and Allyson - Thank you for listening to me ramble, for reading and rereading every book, and for helping me to create. I'd be lost without you.

Candi Kane PR – You are amazing. Thank you for handling the PR for this series with such expertise.

Wander & Forest – Thank you for giving Mason the perfect look.

A special thank you to every blogger and reader who took the time to take part in the cover reveal and release day.

Love ya all tons ;)

Printed in Great Britain
by Amazon